D0952256

WHEN CHRISTMAS COMES

WHEN CHRISTMAS COMES

A Yuletide Mystery

ANDREW KLAVAN

THE MYSTERIOUS PRESS
NEW YORK

WHEN CHRISTMAS COMES

Mysterious Press
An Imprint of Penzler Publishers
58 Warren Street
New York, N.Y. 10007

First Mysterious Press edition

Interior design by Maria Fernandez

Library of Congress Control Number: 2021916052

Cloth ISBN: 978-1-61316-240-8
Ebook ISBN: 978-1-61316-241-5

10 9 8 7 6 5 4 3 2 1

Printed in the United States of America
Distributed by W. W. Norton & Company

This book is for Owen and Zaidee Brennan.

"Faithful friends who are dear to us."

"The past is a foreign country."

—L. P. Hartley, *The Go-Between*

PROLOGUE

Beneath the snow, beside the lake, just at the fall of evening, the little city looked like a dream of home, a long-lost home fondly remembered. Even from a distance, seen from a nearby hill, the colored Christmas lights were visible on the trees that lined the main avenue. Decorations on some bright houses in the surrounding neighborhoods twinkled and beamed. And when the streetlamps came on at the first deep touch of dusk, the core of the town rose sweetly out of the shadows, silver and gold.

"In the midst of a rapidly changing America, Sweet Haven looks like a picture from the past," said a man's voice over the image. "A Christmas card from a simpler time."

The camera drew back and the man who was speaking appeared onscreen. He was a young man with fine blond hair, a TV reporter from the state capital. He was dressed in a dark winter coat and wore a tartan scarf around his neck. His cheeks were pink with the cold. He spoke into a microphone he held in his hand as he stood with the city laid out behind him, a picturesque backdrop.

"Just twenty miles away from the US Army's Fort Anderson, Sweet Haven is a bastion of patriotism and old-fashioned values where many active and retired military personnel come to settle down and raise their families. But today," he continued, "this sweet haven has been rocked by the arrest of one of its favorite sons."

As the reporter spoke, his image and the image of the city were replaced by video of a man in handcuffs being hustled into a police station by several officers. A crowd of onlookers watched the prisoner pass. All of them looked grim. Some were in tears.

"Travis Blake, a third-generation Army Ranger who was awarded the Silver Star for his heroic actions in Afghanistan, has confessed to brutally murdering his girlfriend, Jennifer Dean, and dumping her body somewhere in the thousand cubic miles of this great lake."

When the reporter said the name of the murder victim, her photograph appeared. The man watching the TV report drew a sharp breath and sat up straighter on the sofa. In the dark room, only the light from the television made his face visible. It was a cruel face; soulless; the face of an assassin.

"Dean, a beloved school librarian at Sweet Haven Elementary School, had been dating Blake for several months, but police say the relationship deteriorated when Blake became obsessively jealous."

Now, Will Sherrin, the chief of the city's police force, appeared onscreen, standing behind a podium. He was a tall, broad-shouldered white man, fit but beginning to run soft around the middle. He was addressing a roomful of reporters. Other police brass stood behind him. All the men had a distinctly military presence. All of them seemed somber and upset at having to arrest one of their own.

"Travis is a man we all know," Chief Sherrin said. "We all knew his father and respected him. Like a lot of people in this country, the family has had some real bad times, and it hit Travis hard. We thought—we hoped—that Travis's relationship with Miss Dean would bring him out of his dark place. But I guess it didn't turn out that way. It's just a tragedy."

The reporter came back on the screen, the dusk deeper around him, the little city brighter in the distance behind him.

"Now," he said, "as the Christmas season begins, this peaceful little town will watch one of its heroes brought before a judge, where he faces a sentence of life in prison without parole."

With that, the reporter vanished. The town vanished. The whole scene was gone. The man watching from the sofa had lifted the remote and pressed the power button. With the TV off, the room was draped in almost total blackness. Only the distant lights of Los Angeles coming through the window glinted on the watcher's eyes—his brutal eyes—and glinted, too, on the black metal of the Beretta 9 mm semiautomatic pistol he was gripping expertly in one hand.

PART ONE

A PLOT AGAINST TIME

Christmas never meant much to me after Charlotte went away. Charlotte brought the season into my life and I guess you could say she took it with her when she left. Still, whenever Christmas comes, I think of her.

We met when we were both children, me seven, she nine or so. I wasn't a very happy boy. "A grim presence," my father once called me. And I suppose I was. Serious. Silent. Watchful. Sad. Melancholy *might be the word for it.*

My father worked in the financial sector, whatever that means. I never quite knew what he did for a living. I never had to learn. He inherited a fortune and he turned it into a bigger fortune, that's all I know. As for my mother, she dabbled in things, little arts and crafts projects that she would occasionally try to turn into a business. We had a town house in the city and a mansion out by the water. I had private tutors and flew on private jets and had private birthday parties in toy stores and theme parks rented out for the purpose.

A poor little rich boy, that's what I was. Truly, what I remember most about it is the loneliness. Those birthday parties—children would come—"Your friends," my mother would call them—but I never knew who any of them were. My parents had no time for me. Whenever they would come upon me in one of the rooms, they always looked startled, as if they'd completely forgotten I lived in the same house with them. If my mother came upon me by myself, a look of absolute panic would come into her eyes. She would ask, "Where's Nanny?" in this strained, high-pitched, near-hysterical voice. And when Nanny would return from wherever she was, mother would breathe an enormous sigh of relief. "Oh! There she is!" Clearly, for a moment, she had been terrified she was going to have to figure out how to mother me on her own.

From the time I was five years old or so, Nanny was a homely little German woman named Mia Shaefer. She had only come to America a few months before we hired her. She and her family had gotten out of the eastern sector after the Soviet Union collapsed and the wall came down.

She was a small, slender, quiet, silver-haired spinster. Her Teutonic rigidity and precision were softened by a rich reserve of maternal tenderness and a sly sense of humor, teasing but gentle. I could never love her like she deserved because she was not my mother. I was holding my love back, you see, in the hopes my mother would come around and realize, on second thought, she really did want to tend to me, after all.

But Mia was all I had, and she was devoted to me, and whether I knew it or not, whether I appreciated it or not, her nurturing kindness, I would even say her love, was all the meat and drink on which my child's heart was fed.

So anyway, I was talking about Christmas. It was a pretty miserable affair at my house. My parents were not at all religious, so there was nothing to it, to begin with, no underlying substance, I mean. It was mostly just elaborate decorations, all white on white, for some reason. And night after night there were fashionable parties to which I was never invited. There were plenty of presents on the day, of course, but what did I need presents for? I already had everything. In truth, my earliest memory of the holiday is me sitting in my room one year, watching some musical Christmas special on television and dreaming I was there, inside the TV, standing on the vaguely Victorian set, caroling under the fake snowfall. I wanted to be a member of the family of singers in their colorful sweaters and woolly hats.

Then, one Christmas, my parents received an invitation to spend the holidays with some friends in England. These were very lofty folk, as I understand it. True aristocrats with titles and everything. One of them was even a confidante of some member of the royal family.

Well, my mother was a very charming and elegant lady, but underneath all that, she was just a middle-class girl from the Midwest. And she was always a bit of a social climber, dazzled by high society. So this, for her, was like being invited to heaven. And the last thing she wanted was to have me along, getting in the way.

So off I was sent to spend the holidays with Mia and her family. "Won't that be fun?" my mother said.

And you know what? It really was fun. More fun, I think, than I had ever had in my life.

Mia lived in a small suburb about half an hour out of the city. The houses were modest there but fiercely respectable. Lawns mown. Windows washed. This was a neighborhood of people who had got a fingerhold on the middle class and they weren't going to let go of it come hell or high water.

Mia's house was a small two-story gray-shingled dwelling on a patch of grass in a close row of houses much like it. She lived there with her family, all refugees from the old Communist world. There was her older sister, Klara, who worked as an aide at a local hospital: a cranky fussbudget but with a kind heart. There was their younger brother, Albert, a stalwart, down-to-earth, trustworthy sort of fellow, a security guard at an office building in town. Albert was a widower. As I understood it, his wife had died before they all came over to the US. But he had a daughter, and she was there too. That was Charlotte.

It's no exaggeration to say that Charlotte was the most beautiful creature I had ever seen till then or have ever seen since. Blond and slim and prim with perfect features and bottomless blue eyes. She looked like one of those china figurines Mia and Klara collected and displayed everywhere about the house. I'm sure you've seen the sort of thing: angelic Bavarian children in lederhosen and dirndls. Charlotte looked like one of them.

But I don't think that's why I fell in love with her at first sight the way I did. It wasn't just that anyway.

It was because she was so much like Mia—exactly like Mia really, only I didn't have to withhold my heart from her because she wasn't there to replace my mother like Mia was. Aside from that fact, she was a miniature of the original: a serious and precise little housewife, always busy with something, doing everything just so with the most serious perfectionism, yet with the same warm maternal tenderness in her eyes that Mia had and the same small teasing smile at the corner of her mouth too. I adored her almost from the moment I first saw her.

As soon as I arrived, I was put to work alongside Albert. We brought home a tree together, strung it with drugstore lights and crowded it with dime-store decorations. We assembled a train set on a card table in the front parlor, and set the locomotive going round and round a plastic German village that we arranged near the tracks then decked with Styrofoam snow. We hauled in wood and Albert taught me how to build a fire in the fireplace.

All the while, Mia and Klara and Charlotte were in the kitchen baking Christmas cookies and roasting lamb and potatoes. Charlotte was adorable in her pristine apron, and the smell was heavenly. The music was heavenly too. I loved the music. They had a portable compact disc player hooked up to a pair of third-rate speakers and it filled the place with a steady stream of cheesy, sentimental carols sung by crooners from the last generation. I thought every song was fabulously beautiful.

More than anything, though, I was swept away by the palpable family warmth in that place. With my parents, everything was all rush and importance. There was always this sort of sophisticated, dutiful politeness and restraint among us. We spoke pleasantly. We nodded to one another with thin, cold smiles. But here, at Mia's house, there was teasing and nagging and squabbling and constant hilarity. The ladies treated us gentlemen like a cross between slaves and royalty. On the one hand, they were always ordering us about, sending us off on one chore after another, one more trip to the shops to pick up something they'd forgotten. On the other hand, they couldn't do enough for us. They were forever bringing us snacks and drinks. We would sit like kings as they laid out meals for us, and when we were done eating, they would command us to sit still and relax while they cleared the table and washed the dishes.

Albert received both the ladies' bossing and their ministrations with patient good humor. Judging by the gleam in his eye, he considered himself the luckiest man in the world. He was loved, that was for certain. Charlotte particularly idolized him. Whatever she accomplished, she wanted to show Papa. "Papa, look what I've done!" And whenever it was time to put a plate or a glass before him, she begged her aunts to let her be the one to do the job.

After dinner each night, Albert would ensconce himself in the plush armchair by the living room fire. He'd light a pipe and read the paper and sometimes drink a beer. And when it was bedtime—Charlotte's bedtime and mine—we would come in and sit cross-legged at his feet, and he would lay the paper aside and turn the ceaseless music low and tell us a story. They were good stories, I remember, though it was all I could do to pay attention when I was so distracted by Charlotte's beauty—her perfect face turned up to her father with an expression of near-religious devotion. The firelight lay an unsteady blush on her cheeks and set a sparkle flickering in her blue eyes. I could not stop stealing glances at her.

I do remember this one story Albert told us, though. I remember it almost word for word, in fact. I think he told it on Christmas Eve. Yes, it was Christmas Eve, because I remember we had gone to church before dinner. That was my first time at church, and it had filled me with a sense of awe and solemnity. I remember when Charlotte and I gathered around Albert's chair, he leaned down to us where we sat on the floor—leaned down, holding his pipe up by his ear so the smoke wouldn't get in our faces—leaned down and with his expression serious but his eyes laughing, said in his thick German accent, "Now lieblinge, *on Christmas Eve, you know, it is impossible we do not tell a ghost story. What do you think? Will we be too frightened of it?"*

We children shuddered but solemnly shook our heads no. I could almost taste the thrill I felt: delicious.

These events happened, Albert said, when he was a very young man, working for the Vopos, the People's Police in the city of Brandenburg on the River Havel. It was a Christmas Eve, he told us, much like this very one, dark and cold and snowy as it was just then as he was telling the story. A thick mist had risen from the river and was curling through the narrow, cobbled streets of the city. The streets were white and wet and all of them empty as midnight neared, as the people lay in bed, waiting for Christmas morning.

Only he, only Albert, was walking in the mist, no light but his dim yellow flashlight to guide him. His footfalls on the cobbles echoed through the emptiness. He was cold and wet from the snow, and eager to finish his rounds and head home to a bowl of soup and his warm bed.

But as he passed through the darker shadows beneath an archway, he felt a chill on the back of his neck. He had a sudden sense that there was someone behind him.

"I turned to look," he told us, "holding up my flashlight, but the beam barely made a way through the gloom at all and I could see nothing."

After a while, he walked on, emerging onto a narrow lane winding uphill. But now, he had more than just a sense that someone was following him.

"I heard footsteps!"

He could hear someone walking behind him, not far off, moving when he moved, stopping whenever he stopped.

He turned again and raised his flashlight again. "Who's there?" he called into the mist and the swirling snow.

At first there was no reply. But then, very dimly, Albert heard something. Faintly first. Then louder, closer.

Someone was weeping. A girl.

"I called again," he told us, leaning down toward where we sat at his feet. "And now, there they were again, yes? The footsteps. And as I stood there watching, a shape began to come toward me out of the swirling white that filled that black, black Christmas Eve so long ago."

He saw a silhouette. He heard the sound of weeping grow louder.

"Hello. What is the matter?" he called.

The weeping grew louder still. The silhouette became a shape, the shape became a solid figure. It was the figure of a young woman.

As Albert stood and stared, the woman finally stepped out of the mist and into the light where he could see her clearly.

Albert had been about to call again, but he fell silent at the sight of her, his mouth hanging open.

The girl before him was only sixteen or so, he told us. She was very lovely, but her long brown hair fell all bedraggled around her tearstained face and she was dressed—this was what amazed him—in nothing but a stained white shift, which could give her no protection at all from the damp and the cold.

"Mein Gott! Are you not freezing, fräulein?" Albert said. "What are you doing out so late? Where do you live?"

She answered only his last question. "My place is on the hill on the far side of the trees," she said. She sniffled and swiped the tears from her cheeks.

"Through the park here?" asked Albert—pointing in the direction of a little wood nearby.

The girl nodded.

"Well, then, come," said Albert, "and I will take you home."

With another nod, she agreed, and they began to walk together side by side up the hill toward the park.

"What is your name?" he asked her.

"Adelina. Adelina Weber," she said.

"Are you not cold, Adelina?"

"Very cold."

He took off his overcoat and draped it over her shoulders. She clutched it closed around her neck and shivered.

"Very cold," she said again.

They walked on in silence. He had a feeling she did not want to talk, and yet as a policeman, he felt he had to find out how she had come to be here in this condition.

They came to the park. They entered a pathway between the trees, the stark, naked trees, white with snow all around them.

He felt compelled to break their silence. "Why are you out in the night alone like this, fräulein?" he asked her after a while. "Dressed like this, almost nothing on?"

The girl had stopped crying now. She simply grasped the coat's collar and stared forlornly into the mist that shifted around them.

"I came out to meet my love," she said.

"I see."

"Johann."

"Johann. And where is this Johann now?"

"He ran away."

"He ran away from you?" said Albert, glancing at her with surprise.

She shook her head. "He ran away from my father."

"Ah, your father found you, then."

She nodded but resolutely said nothing. Albert sensed it was best to stop questioning her for a few moments.

They walked in silence. The path beneath the trees began to climb more steeply. Soon they were out of the forest and moving together up a rising lane lined with houses. Through the mist, Albert began to make out the distinctive shape of a Gothic church at the crest of the hill. As they climbed, he could see its oddly shaped tower all of red brick. It was a square tower for most of its length but became circular at the top and was then crowned by a conical brass steeple, green with verdigris. The structure loomed darkly out of the night-whiteness.

Finally, Albert repeated his question: "So your father found you—found you with Johann?"

The girl answered mournfully, "It was Johann who gave us away. It was something he said in my father's hearing. I don't know what. But my father followed me from the house when I snuck out, and he found us together."

Albert waited for her to go on, but she didn't. He pressed her: "He was angry with you, then? Your father? Did he tell you that you could not come home?" He was beginning to wonder if he was going to have to settle a domestic dispute before he could finish his shift tonight.

But the girl only responded softly, "Here we are."

She stopped—and Albert stopped. They had reached the top of the hill. But there were no dwellings nearby. They were standing instead before the low wall that surrounded the churchyard. The Gothic tower frowned down at them out of the snowfall.

Confused, Albert looked around, his eyes passing over the old slanted headstones in the yard.

Beside him, the girl said quietly, "He did not send me away. My father. He did not send me away. He had a knife. He stabbed me. He stabbed me in the heart."

Albert whipped around to look at her—and he stood there stupefied in the falling snow.

The girl was gone. His overcoat now sat on the stones at his feet, empty, crumpled but still half upright, as if the girl had melted away from within it.

He called her name—"Adelina!"—but there was no answer—no answer but the wind. He began to shiver. Without his coat on, he was freezing. He was afraid he would catch a chill and become sick. Still shouting for her, he recovered his overcoat and slipped it on. He continued calling for her another quarter of an hour, but there was no answer. No sign of her. She had simply vanished.

At last, he was forced to give up and go home.

It was only the next morning that he found her, when he returned to the church, when he walked through the churchyard, when he stood among the old medieval graves.

It was only then he saw the decaying stone that bore her name: Adelina Weber.

The stone stood at the head of the grave where she had been buried after her father murdered her—more than two hundred years before.

1

With that, Cameron Winter turned away and his voice trailed off into silence. For a long moment, Margaret Whitaker simply sat still and looked at him across the little space that separated his chair from hers.

Margaret was sixty-seven. She had been a psychotherapist for almost forty years. She had seen a lot, heard even more, and she considered herself an excellent judge of character. But this man—this man was a mystery to her.

He was handsome, she thought. Quite handsome really—or at least, he had the sort of looks that she had always favored. At her age, the heyday in her blood was tame, as Shakespeare might have said, but she could still feel the sensual appeal of Winter's presence. He was in his mid-thirties. Only average height, but muscular and well formed, broad shouldered, narrow waisted. His face was ethereal, otherworldly, but strong and masculine. It was the face of an angel in a Renaissance painting, she thought, with the golden hair to go with it, wavy and long, tumbling down around his ears. He wore wire-rimmed glasses and a tweed jacket with elbow patches—the uniform of a college professor, which is what he said he was. But there was something about him that was anything but professorial. Something in his sorrowful but watchful eyes. Something in the strength and readiness of his hands. Something . . . Margaret thought.

"Why did you tell me that story?" she asked him. She was genuinely curious.

He was gazing thoughtfully out her office window—out at the short street of stores and taverns twinkling with colored Christmas lights below, at the white dome of the capitol building at the end of the block, at the delicate December snow tumbling over the river beyond. He remained like that, presenting his fine profile to her, even as he murmured: "I couldn't sleep that night. After Albert told the story, I mean. I was already excited for Christmas morning, and now I was afraid too, thinking about the ghost of that murdered girl in the empty city in the snow. I lay awake, tossing and turning, scanning the shadows for terrifying specters. I was yearning to call out for Mia, my nanny, to have her come and comfort me. But I was afraid Charlotte would hear. I couldn't bear the thought that Charlotte would see me for the scared little boy I was."

He faced her—and Margaret felt the power of his attraction again, felt a warm flush travel down the length of her. *Goodness!* she thought mildly.

"But she did hear," he said. "Charlotte must've heard me turning in the sheets. After a while, the door to my bedroom slowly swung in. I lay there staring into the light from the hall, expecting the ghost of Adelina Weber to enter any minute. Instead, in came little Charlotte, serious, motherly, nine-year-old Charlotte. She didn't say a word. Not a word. She just sat down on the edge of my bed. She just sat there and patted my hand and hushed me quietly until I fell asleep."

In the silence that followed, Margaret forced herself not to avert her eyes from his sad, humorous, sensual gaze.

"People come to me when they have problems, Cameron," she said.

"Of course. I know that," he answered.

"You say so. But you come into my office and you sit down and you start telling me this story, and I still have no idea why you're here."

He lifted his chin a little and considered it. "I'm here . . ." he began, and then paused as if searching for the right word. "I'm here because I'm sad," he said finally.

"You're depressed, you mean."

"I'm—melancholy. All the time. More and more every day."

"Yes," said Margaret. "I can see that."

"Can you?" he said, surprised.

"Yes. And you think it may have something to do with this Christmas you spent at your nanny's house?"

He shrugged. "It came into my mind. Looking out the window at the snow and the Christmas lights, I just suddenly remembered it. I thought I was supposed to tell you whatever came into my head."

"No, I'm not that sort of therapist."

"Ah. Sorry."

"Tell me more, though. About your melancholy. What about your work? Have you lost interest in your work?" Margaret asked. "You said you were a professor at the university."

"An associate professor. In English literature. The English Romantic poets. A dying subject—and yes, that does depress me somewhat: the fact that it's dying."

"What about sex?"

"That's kind of you, but it seems unethical under the circumstances."

She gave him the thin smile she always gave male clients when they made that joke, or one like it. "Have you lost interest in sex?" she repeated.

He sighed. "No. Sex is fine. It's relationships I've lost interest in. My body does what bodies do, but the soul has gone out of it. The meaning. Why do you keep glancing at my hands?"

The sudden question caught Margaret off guard. She was a close and expert observer, but most of her clients were too fascinated by their own problems and predicaments to observe her observing them.

She paused a moment before answering. She allowed her observations about his hands to coalesce. The callouses on the edges, the slight swelling of the first two knuckles—she'd seen such things before. They were from striking wood, from doing push-ups with fists pressed into asphalt. The man was a serious martial artist of some sort. Not a sportsman. A real fighter. For the first time, her impression of him spoke itself clearly into her mind: she was sitting in her office with a dangerous man, a man capable of hurting people. She did not think he would hurt her. He wasn't a criminal. It wasn't that. But he didn't have the bearing of a military man either. So then what—what was he?

The silence had gone on too long. Aloud, she said, "They're not a professor's hands, are they?"

He seemed to consider her. He gave a soft grunt. "Have you heard about me on the news?"

"I don't follow the news," she said. "I find it too upsetting."

"You didn't look me up? You didn't hear about the kidnapping in the lake country? Or about those children who went missing during the recent riots?"

Margaret shook her head.

Her office was decorated in various shades of brown and tan: the carpet, the furniture, the wallpaper. There were photographs hung here and there of serene country settings: a sunset on the water, wildflowers in a field. Everything was designed to communicate tranquility. But now, the handsome, tweedy Cameron Winter changed positions in his chair, merely shifted from one position to another, and all that carefully constructed tranquility was shattered by the rhythmic self-control of his movements and the coiled violence it implied.

"I have," he told her mildly, "a strange habit of mind."

"Oh?"

"I hear about things. Things people tell me. Stories in the news. Or I read about things online somewhere. And sometimes, I can think my way into them. Imagine my way into them, as if I'm there. And because of that, I begin to discern the causes of events when other people can't."

"You're talking about . . ."

"Crimes, mostly," he said. "Acts of evil. Sometimes, if I think them through in just the right way, I can help find the people responsible for acts of evil."

All these decades, all the clients she had treated, all the stories she had heard of horror and abuse, and still Margaret found she had to clear her throat before she could ask him: "And what do you do to these evil people when you find them?"

Cameron Winter smiled.

2

After he left Margaret Whitaker's office, Winter headed down the street in the direction of the capitol building. He had his hands shoved deep in his brown shearling coat and his ivy cap pulled low on his brow as he bulled his way through the snowfall. He seemed, indeed, a grim presence. But in fact, for the first time in months, he felt a small, tremulous lightness inside him, a candle in the inner darkness so to speak. It had been some long while since he had liked or respected someone as much as he liked and respected the therapist. He felt a faint sense of hope. It might well be that she could find a way to relieve him of the burden of his sorrow.

He peeked up from under his cap at the red and green and white and yellow lights in the storefronts, the cutouts and frost-drawings of angels and Santa Claus, the wreaths and the plastic pines. Again, he thought of Charlotte, thought of her not as he had seen her last, thank God, but as he had spoken of her in the office just now: the little housewife, sitting on his bed, patting his child hand with her child hand until he slept.

He shook the memory off like a dog shaking off water. Back to the present, he thought. Back to the murder of Jennifer Dean.

He pushed through the door of the Nomad Tavern and stepped gratefully into the warmth of the place. Dark wood everywhere, the bars and the tables. State flags spread over the pressed tin ceiling. An elaborate but somehow homey mosaic floor. Lots of government paper pushers finishing their lunches here, overcoats draped over chairs, televisions hung above them on the wall, sports interviews playing silently.

Victoria Nowak was sitting alone in the corner—waiting for him there as she sometimes used to do back in the old days when they were violating the laws of God and man with their student-teacher affair. He mentally corrected himself as he approached her. She was married now. She was Victoria Grossburger.

Victoria smiled, and her eyes openly appraised him as he swept his cap off and bent down to kiss her cheek. He settled into the chair across from her.

"God, look at you. You're so handsome it hurts," she said.

"I thought you loved me for my mind, Vic."

"Ach, I never loved you for your mind. Your mind is terrifying."

"Yet here you are," he said.

She had not changed much in the years since he'd seen her last. Well, she had lost the spectacular allure of youth, of course, but she still had an appealingly vivacious and cheerful aspect. Sparkling eyes under a tumble of black curls. A sweet, optimistic face, complete with freckles. The look of a high school girl who believed good things would happen in her life. Plus she had a wonderfully generous shape that could still light a fire in him, if he gave it the chance.

He didn't. He flagged the waitress. Ordered a coffee. Vic already had hers.

"So you're in Sweet Haven now, up by the lake?" he said.

She nodded. "Roger—my husband—is just finishing up his service as an instructor at Fort Anderson. We knew we'd be there for a year or so, so I thought I'd take a job nearby and there was an opening in the public defender's office. I'm half the legal staff, one of two."

"How do you like it?"

She tilted her head, considering. "It's nice. Very nice. I guess."

"You're not sure."

"Sweet Haven is a peculiar place. A particular place, let's say. It couldn't be any more lovely as a setting. The lake. The hills. The old-fashioned all-American architecture. The whole place has an old-fashioned feeling—in a good way. Wholesome. Quaint. Good values. The sort of place you want to settle down and raise a family."

"But?"

"Well, not *but*, just . . . The base—Fort Anderson—is maybe twenty miles away. It's one of only four bases that house the Rangers, the Army's special operations force. Over the years, soldiers served there, maybe met a local girl, got married, and moved to Sweet Haven when they got out. Then they'd have kids, and their kids would join the Army, become Rangers. Then they'd meet a girl and so on. The result is . . . well, strange."

"Strange like provincial?" Winter asked.

The waitress brought his coffee and refilled Vic's. They both drank and their eyes met over the rims of their cups. For a moment all the memories between them—all the things they weren't saying to each other—were silently said.

Then Victoria set her cup down in its saucer with a rattle. She looked away from him and went on.

"The Rangers are an elite unit, the best of the best," she said. "They're well-educated, physically trained up the hoo-ha. Mostly white, but it's a brotherhood, you know, so if you get in, you're one of them, no matter who you are. So many of the men in Sweet Haven have served over the years that the whole town is sort of shaped like them, if you see what I mean. The men all have a similar look, similar haircuts, the same way of walking, talking, even thinking. The cops, the lawyers, the businessmen—almost every male, it seems like, is an ex-Ranger. It affects the women too, in their way. They're all those cheerful, no-nonsense, take-care-of-everything, all-American military wives. It's not bad, it's just a little bit eerie, like a town full of clones."

Winter smiled as he lifted his coffee cup again.

"The men remind me of you a little actually," Victoria said. "But you were never in the military, were you?"

"Tell me about Travis Blake," said Winter. "You're defending him?"

"No. There is no defense. He already pled guilty. Sentencing is scheduled for the last Monday before the holiday."

"The girl he killed, Jennifer Dean, that was his girlfriend, right?"

"Right. The school librarian. Everyone loved her. He loved her, everyone says."

"But he pled, he confessed. He says he did it."

"Oh, he did it, all right," said Victoria. "People saw her driving up to his house. No one else was there. Travis's daughter, Lila, was staying overnight with a friend. When Jennifer didn't show up for work the next morning, the police went up to Travis's place. The crime scene guys found Jennifer's blood on the carpet. Traces of her blood on Travis's combat knife. A security camera at the marina caught Travis on video hauling a rolled rug down to his sailboat. The rug wasn't big enough. When they enhance the picture, blow it up, you can actually see Jennifer's body inside."

"You can identify her?"

"Definitely. Later that night, he was spotted driving her car out toward the river. That's on video too, and there's also three eyewitnesses. Police dragged the water, found the car. Two weeks later, they arrested him."

Mid-sip of coffee, Winter raised an eyebrow, surprised. "Two weeks? What took them so long?"

Victoria's face wasn't made for sad smiles, which made it all the sadder to see. "The guy is Sweet Haven royalty," she said. "His grandfather was in the First Ranger Battalion in Italy during World War II. His father was a Ranger in 'Nam. He, the father, was the one who made the move to Sweet Haven. He made a pile in real estate and started a horse farm on the edge of town. Travis grew up in the classic Big House on the Hill. Columns on the portico, acres of rolling green, the whole deal. He could have had an easy life. He could have been the soft one, the spoiled one, the heir ruined by wealth. But nope, when he got out of Dartmouth, he enlisted in the Army and became—what else?—a Ranger. And he was a stone hero in Afghanistan, Cam. He got a Silver Star for single-handedly defending a landing zone while under heavy fire. He held off the evildoers for nearly forty-five minutes so the choppers could come in and rescue his wounded comrades—twenty-five of them. He saved twenty-five lives."

"So no one wanted to believe he was guilty," Winter said.

She sighed. "The top cops are all ex-Rangers. The prosecutor. All the rank and file cops are ex-Army, even the guards in the jail are. They'd have rather handcuffed their own mothers than bring Travis in. When the detectives came up to the Big House to get him, they actually apologized for the inconvenience of putting him under arrest. You know what Travis said? He said, 'It's okay, fellas. I did it.' "

"Did he say why?"

"As much as he says anything, which isn't much. I mean, I'm his defense and he'll barely talk to me. But from what I can gather, he became obsessed with the idea there was another man in her life. Everyone agrees she was a very secretive person. She wouldn't talk about her past at all. He says it drove him crazy. He kept asking her questions. She kept refusing to answer. They argued. It got violent. He stabbed her."

"Sad story."

"It tore the town apart. Not just because of him. Because of her too. She was a relative newcomer, but she'd already become a beloved figure in the town herself. Everyone's crushed."

Winter had finished his coffee now. He held up a hand at the waitress to keep her from bringing him a refill. He sat back in his chair, folded his hands on his stomach. His eyes played over Victoria and she let them, coloring a little.

"It's good to see you, Vic," he said.

She nodded. "To be honest with you? I wasn't prepared for how good it would be."

"Things are okay, though? With the marriage. With Ralph."

"Roger."

"Roger. That's what I meant."

She smiled. It really did move him, the familiar smile, the look of her. Like her, he was surprised by how strong the old attraction was. Maybe he wasn't as dead inside as he thought.

"The marriage is good," she said finally. "The deployment was tough. He saw a lot of action. But he's back and he'll be out soon and . . . it's good between us now. Really good."

"Good," he said, still watching her. "So? Why did you call me?"

"I read about you solving the kidnapping. And those missing kids. How you showed up out of nowhere and tracked down the bad guys. I remembered how you used to read the news, the crime stories. How you used to tell me what you thought really happened. You always said you had . . ."

She couldn't find the words, so he reminded her: "A strange habit of mind."

"A strange habit of mind, that's it."

"But still, I don't see how I can help here. You've got the evidence. The confession. The case seems pretty straightforward. What do you need me to do?"

She pinned him with a look that went deep. He didn't know if she planned to get at him that way or it just happened. But it did happen, and he already knew he would move heaven and earth to do whatever impossible thing she was about to ask of him.

She leaned forward, looked in his eyes and said: "I need you to prove he's innocent."

3

The sun was shining when he drove into Sweet Haven, but the rolling lawns were still covered with snow. A vast sky of perfect blue hung over the little city end to end. Victoria had been right. It was a town out of the past. No, out of a dream of the past, out of a time when things were the way they were supposed to be but never really are.

A church tower looked down on neat, well-tended clapboard houses and Victorian manses, all of them dressed up in lights for Christmas. Toward the center of town, office buildings of brick and stone were hung with wreaths and crosses. Winter-coated companions, friends and lovers walked in the park on paths through snowy hills and on stone bridges over the icy river. On the lonely winter beach by the lake, a single man looked out at the vast expanse of glittering water.

Winter saw it all through the windshield of his Jeep SUV. It struck him with a pang of nostalgia. He wondered for the first time if maybe it wasn't the memory of Charlotte that had begun to weigh on him so heavily as Christmas drew near. Maybe Charlotte was just a symbol of something else, something deeper: a sense that the best of his life had been lost irretrievably and the memory of his sins had grown too heavy to bear.

That thought—that the best of life was over, that some sins were not redeemable—naturally brought his mind back to Travis Blake.

Victoria had told him about the ex-Ranger's life after the two of them had left the Nomad Tavern. The snowfall had grown lighter by then, and they had strolled together around the park outside the capitol building. Their shoulders touched just a little too often as Vic unfolded the sad story.

"You can't come back to the country you fought for," Victoria said. "Roger told me that. You can't come back to the life you left behind. Nothing is ever the same. Everything changes. In Travis's case, everything changed for the worse."

When he finished college and joined the Army, Travis was the self-assured, wealthy scion of a successful horse farmer. His family—his mother and father and his sister, May—had never been anything but happy together, a united clan.

At college, Travis had become engaged to Patricia Stanton, a charming and intelligent daughter of the rising middle class. When Travis went off to basic training, Patricia moved to New York and continued her education at Columbia, working toward a PhD in communications. Her hope was to have a career in fundraising for worthy nonprofits. The shape of the life ahead of them seemed clear and they had a lot to look forward to.

Travis barely noticed when the economy went bad. He was in the midst of the grueling eight-week training course known as RASP, the Ranger Assessment and Selection Program. Every last spark and particle of his focus and effort was trained on getting through the brutal gauntlet meant to weed out the unworthy. His father, who remembered what the training was like, didn't want to distract his son with his own problems.

Travis was already in Afghanistan by the time he began to understand that his parents were in financial trouble. He could hear the strain in his mother's voice when he'd call home from the MWR Internet Café in FOB Kalagush. He finally confronted his father, face-to-computerized-face. The old man admitted the truth: they were selling off assets as fast as they could, but it did not look like they would be able to save the farm.

When he came home on leave, he found his family in an uproar. May, who was now in college in Ohio, had announced that she was in love with a woman. Travis rolled his eyes at the news. May had always been a scrappy little troublemaker, so it all made sense to him. But his father was shattered. He couldn't even bring himself to express the depth of the injury May's sexuality had inflicted on his sense of himself and the world. By the time Travis returned to the Stan, his mother and father were at odds and his sister wasn't talking to anyone, not even him. Soon after, his parents retired to Florida. It was a way of escaping the scene of their failure, and also a way of cutting expenses so they could save the Big House, all that was left of their once-vast property.

There were bright spots that obscured the steady decline of Travis's fortunes. He married Patricia when she graduated. She became pregnant and gave birth to a little girl, Lila. She moved to Sweet Haven and lived in the Big House and worked from home as Communications Director for a charity serving wounded veterans.

Travis retired from the service after ten years. His daughter was four by then, and he didn't want to miss any more of her childhood. It was only when he returned home for good that he fully understood the extent of the disaster that had struck him and his family. His father was now sinking into an early old age, railing bitterly against the politicians and the banks who had ruined the economy and the country. His mother had become a weak and weepy character. His sister had gone radical, so pierced and tattooed that, to Travis, she looked like some sort of primitive savage escaped from the Amazon rainforest. And then came the worst, the most heartbreaking discovery: his wife, suffering from intense anxiety in his absence, had been secretly self-medicating. She had become addicted to painkillers.

For Travis at this point, his first concern was his daughter. The serious, contemplative little nubbins had completely colonized his heart. He had not known he could love anyone so much. She was the meaning and purpose of his life. He had taken a job with an executive relocation firm, but when he came to realize his wife could no longer take care of the child, he gave up his job to become a stay-at-home father. With the help of occasional consulting work, he lived on the trust fund his parents had been too honorable to touch.

Then came the final blow. Travis had just wrangled his wife into rehab for the third time. One stormy night, as the lightning came in off the lake in a purple mist, Patricia threw a chair through the rehab facility's fifth-floor window then dove through the jagged opening, falling to her death on the pavement below.

"Quite a string of misfortunes," Winter remarked mildly.

"It was downright gothic, if you ask me," Victoria said. "It broke him. He just went dark. Even his buddies couldn't reach him or talk him through. He holed himself up in the Big House. He had only the one horse left, his own horse, this black stallion, Midnight. People would see him riding over the country in the mornings like the devil from hell was chasing him. They thought he was trying to get himself thrown, trying to kill himself, to die."

"Ah, but he couldn't die," said Winter.

"Right. The child."

The girl, Lila, was the only thing he cared about, the only thing he lived for.

Until he fell in love with Jennifer Dean.

4

Winter reached his hotel. It was a three-story clapboard colonial inn, archaic and charming like the town itself, redolent of a fanciful American past. As he climbed the front stairs to the long front porch, he thought how fine it would be to plant himself in one of the rockers out there and spend an hour or so peering at lake water to the horizon.

A sweet, soft choral rendition of "Silent Night" greeted him as he checked in, followed him up in the elevator to the top floor, and then—coming now from the TV on the wall—segued into "Adeste Fidelis" as he unpacked in the large, bright, comfortable room with its picture window looking out at the lake.

When he finished putting his clothes away, he went back downstairs and out to his Jeep. He drove over to the elementary school where Jennifer Dean had been the librarian.

It was a soulless little fortress of a brick building, closed up for the holiday. The principal, Nichola Atwater, had said she was doing some work in her office and would meet him there.

He found himself walking down empty halls, his footsteps echoing. The walls were papered with crayon drawings of square houses with triangle roofs and zigzag Christmas trees nearby. He tried to laugh off his absurd feeling that the building, deserted for Christmas, somehow missed its children.

"It feels like the building is lonely, doesn't it?"

Startled to hear his thoughts spoken out loud, he looked up and saw the principal waiting for him outside her office at the end of the hall.

"It feels like the school misses its children," she said.

So maybe it was not such an absurd feeling, after all, Winter thought.

It may have been that Victoria had conditioned him to see the strangeness of Sweet Haven. It may have been that she had put the image in his mind of a clone city, everyone the same. But glancing out his car windows as he'd driven through town, he had noticed the military bearing of many of the men on the street, straight and yet easy, confident and yet watchful and yet self-secure.

Now, as he approached Mrs. Atwater, he felt certain at once that she had been a military wife. What had Victoria said of them? They were "cheerful, no-nonsense, take-care-of-everything, all-American" women. True enough, but there was more to it than that, another level. Mrs. Atwater was a slender, elegant, bright-eyed woman of fifty, with short, gray-and-black hair over an attractive face the color of café au lait. What marked her as government issue, Winter thought, was the poised femininity on the outside hiding an antic sense of irony within. "Humankind cannot bear very much reality," the poet said. Military wives bore a lot of reality—from mind-boggling bureaucracy to constant relocations to sudden widowhood—and they either developed an antic sense of irony or grew bitter and night-dark inside.

"We'll go to the library," she told him. "That was her place. It's the best place to talk about her."

They walked side by side down the lonesome hall, past the walls crowded with crayon drawings of happy Christmas scenes.

"So you work for Travis's lawyer, is that right?" said Mrs. Atwater as they went.

"I do," said Winter.

"Hasn't he confessed to it all?"

"He has. But because he confessed without a plea deal, his sentence hasn't been determined. If there are any mitigating factors, we want to make sure the judge knows about them."

Winter could not tell what Mrs. Atwater thought about that, whether it made her angry to think that Blake might be treated leniently or whether she had some fondness or compassion for him. She was a woman who had clearly had practice in keeping her thoughts to herself.

"Jennifer's murder was a terrible thing," she went on, firmly but without any hint of hostility. "One of the worst things that's ever happened here. I can't tell you how it broke our hearts. We all loved her so much. She had a sort of magic about her. Maybe that sounds trite, but we all experienced it. We would talk about it, even before . . . what happened. I saw it from the first moment she arrived. Out of nowhere really. Before we'd even advertised the position. I was talking to the old librarian, Mrs. Gibbs, asking her about her plans, and I looked up and there she was, Jennifer, standing in the doorway. She said, 'I heard you were looking for a new librarian.' She had been asking around town apparently. But she was just so perfect for the job, it felt like magic."

"She wasn't from Sweet Haven, then."

"Oh no. To be honest, none of us ever knew where she was from. I mean, we had her résumé, but we never knew where she was from originally. She said she was coming out of a bad relationship and made it clear that it was painful for her to answer personal questions about the past. After a while, we just stopped asking." She raised her slender shoulders as if to shrug off any regrets she had about this. "She had an accent, though. Very faint. Russian, I think, though somehow she never got around to telling me about that either. But when she died—did they tell you this?—the police spent days trying to find her next of kin. No one came forward. They even put her face out on social media for a day or two. It made some of the news outlets but still . . . no one claimed her."

"Yes, I read that. It's strange—given that you all loved her so much, you'd think there'd be others who would have too."

"Yes," said Mrs. Atwater thoughtfully. Then she said, "She was—I'm not sure how best to describe it—a receiving presence, not a giving one. *You* talked to *her*. She listened. Pretty soon, you found you had told her everything about yourself—and you felt better for it too. She had a wonderful, soothing way about her. But *she* hadn't told *you* anything, nothing at all.

It made her seem almost—I don't know—ghostlike. Or angel-like. Something like that, something more spirit than flesh."

They came to the library. Mrs. Atwater chose a key from the clutch of them hanging from the narrow belt around her gray dress. As she unlocked the door, Winter said, "Is that what was magic about her? That spiritual quality?"

Mrs. Atwater pushed open the door and held it for him. "I suppose so," she said. "Her quiet. Her stillness. Her sweetness too. She radiated something. Tenderness? Loving-kindness maybe. The children absolutely adored her."

"Given your description, it makes sense that they would."

The door swung shut. They were in a long room now with bookshelves on every wall. Long tables surrounded by child-size chairs. Bright decorations on the wall: large, handmade cut-outs of famous characters from children's books—a boy, a bear, a princess in a castle. Winter, who remembered a childhood when books were his only companions, knew all the characters, all the stories, all of them.

As Mrs. Atwater switched on the lights, he was attracted to a table by the librarian's desk. It held a display of mysteries geared toward little boys. He smiled fondly. Mia used to read these to him. The volumes stood on edge in a semicircle. At the center of the semicircle, lying flat, was a book that was not from the series. Its jacket was adorned with a spectacular and elaborate illustration. It showed a ghostly woman seen through tangled branches. She was standing on a lonely hill with a stately ruined tower beside her and a little village spread below her with a lake beyond. It was an image of deep romance.

"She did that," said Mrs. Atwater, moving behind the librarian's desk.

Winter looked up, surprised. "Jennifer Dean? She drew this?"

"Just at the end. Just before . . . before what happened happened. She illustrated the whole book. Isn't it lovely? She wrote the story too. Then she had it made up in book form just for the children. It's really charming. It's about a ghost in a haunted tower. All the children scare one another telling tales about the horrible things that happened to her during her life and what a horrible, vengeful specter she must be because of them. But when one of the boys is finally brave enough to go into the tower, he finds her spirit is actually very loving and beautiful."

Winter paged through the volume. "These illustrations are amazing."

"Here," said Mrs. Atwater. "This is what I wanted you to see."

She worked the computer keyboard behind the desk, then turned the monitor to face him. A video played: Jennifer Dean, sitting in a wooden chair, reading to a circle of children. The audio was turned down low, but he could hear her faint accent and, yes, Russian it was.

Winter saw at once, too, what the principal had called her magic. Her stillness, her sweetness. She sat almost motionless yet was somehow wonderfully graceful, slim and curved gracefully, only her hands moving—moving gracefully—as she turned each page. She had short hair, black—deep black, blue-black—wedge cut so that it slanted along her rounded jawline, framing her soft, full-cheeked, womanly face. The children gazed up at her with rapt devotion.

Winter heard himself release a long, hollow, unsteady breath.

"Yes," Mrs. Atwater said. "Everyone felt that way about her." She was still speaking without anger when she told him: "I wanted you to see, Mr. Winter. As you go about looking for what you call 'mitigating factors.' I wanted you to understand who it was that Travis Blake stabbed to death."

5

Evening set in early. As the sky darkened to a rich royal blue, Winter drove up to the Big House, Travis's house, thinking about the first time Jennifer had come here.

She had come because of Lila, Mrs. Atwater had told him. Travis Blake's daughter was almost eight now. A silent, thoughtful, motherless little mouse whom none of the other teachers could reach.

She was, though, as all the children were, fascinated with the still, mysterious yet tender presence of the new school librarian. She watched her constantly, like a lover watches her beloved, sometimes sneaking secret glances while bent over a book, sometimes caught out just standing, just gazing as if mesmerized.

Finally, with an instinct she seemed to have of when the moment might be right, Jennifer Dean approached the child, sat across from her in one of the small chairs at one of the library tables. She handed a book to her and said, "Would you read that to me, Lila?"

The book was for a much older child, twelve years old at least, maybe even older than that. But Lila—as Jennifer had somehow known she would—read the words easily and clearly understood them all. When she finished, she looked up expectantly. She did not seem to realize how she had revealed herself.

"You live in the Big House up above Grand Street, don't you?" Jennifer asked her. "The one on the hill on the far side of the river."

Lila nodded solemnly. Her brown eyes never left the librarian's face.

"Where the man on the black horse rides sometimes."

"That's my daddy."

"And where's your mommy?"

"She made herself dead," said Lila.

"I'm sorry. That's so sad."

"It was a long time ago," said the child.

Jennifer phoned Travis Blake twice after that. He didn't answer either time. The first time, she left a message on his voice mail. He didn't call back. The second time she simply cut the connection, waited for a free period, then drove up to confront him in person at the Big House.

Winter arrived there now, at the Big House, his Jeep bouncing up the long, rough driveway. The snow had not been shoveled in a while, but it had been flattened by traffic. Police cars probably, Winter thought. The house was set back from the crest of the hill, and Winter didn't see it until he came over the top. Then there it was, a lowering monster of gray-white stone, neglected, empty. Its walls were banked with old snow. So was the balcony atop the famous columned portico. High mullioned windows, all dark, stared out from three large gables.

God, it was dreary. The windows were like a dead man's eyes. Yellow police tape sealed the front door. It could never have been a cheerful place, Winter thought, not ever. The poor child. Lila, he knew, was with her aunt now, Travis's sister, May, the one with the piercings and crazy hair. But if May had any life or kindness in her at all, Winter thought, wherever they were had to be a sunnier setting for a little girl than this.

It was April when Jennifer Dean had first come here. That was storm season in these parts. Every third day or so, burly, threatening purple fog banks rolled in over the water, turning suddenly, shockingly violet as lightning flashed within them. Rains would follow, pelting and swift. Then, when the rain was over, the fog would linger over the city, leaving everything gloomy and obscure.

There was a fog like that on the hill that day, the day Jennifer Dean drove up here. Winter could only imagine how lonely and eerie it must have felt for her when she stepped out of her ancient, rattletrap Chevy, when she stood shivering in the fog before the fog-draped shadow of the mansion. The rest of the hill would have been all but invisible in the murk. There would have been no noise but the spring branches drip-drip-dripping after the storm.

Even for the taciturn Jennifer, the story of her first meeting with Travis Blake had been too dramatic not to tell. Mrs. Atwater had passed it on to Winter and he—as was his habit—had filled in the details with his own imagination.

Jennifer had knocked on the door. There was no answer. Nervously, tentatively, she tried to open it. It was locked. She turned and peered through the thick and shifting mist. She made out Travis Blake's truck parked in the garage. She had seen the old pickup at the school on the days Blake came to fetch his daughter. If it was here, he was around somewhere, she thought.

She wondered where the stables were, and whether the black horse, Midnight, was in them. She could not see the outbuildings in the fog. She wandered away from the house, searching for them.

She hadn't gone very far—she didn't feel she had gone all that far—when she glanced over her shoulder and discovered her Chevy was no longer visible to her. The house was no longer visible to her. The fog had covered them over.

She was not an easily frightened woman, but a dancing spark of anxiety worked inside her as she realized she had lost her bearings and was not sure of the way back to the driveway. She turned one way and saw mist and turned and saw mist another way. Then she turned a third time.

Out of the fog flew a wild black beast with bared teeth and white eyes rolling. It was there with such supernatural silence and suddenness that it was almost on her before her mind could even take in its presence. She cried out and threw up her hands helplessly as the stallion Midnight reared high above her, the rider roaring like a beast himself and wrestling with the reins.

The horse almost threw him. It almost trampled Jennifer into the earth. But Travis had control again and turned the hooves as they were still flailing. Jennifer fell back a step, her arms still lifted, crossed in front of her face.

Then, with a snort, Midnight settled to the ground. The horse came to a standstill.

One corner of Winter's mouth lifted as he pictured the scene. Victoria had said Travis Blake's life was gothic. Sure enough, this—this dramatic meeting—seemed like something out of Charlotte Brontë. At least it did once he, the English professor, finished reinventing it in his mind.

Breathless, Jennifer had looked up at the horseman through the mist. Travis Blake peered down at her, his mouth twisted in an angry sneer. Midnight snorted, and the fog swirled around his nostrils.

"Who are you?" Travis snarled at her.

Jennifer slowly lowered her arms. She took a longer, deeper breath to steady herself.

"I'm Jennifer Dean. From the school," she said. "I called you. I left a message."

"Ah. Right." The horse danced under him impatiently. "Why are you here?"

"You didn't call me back."

"I didn't want to speak to you."

Jennifer Dean lifted her chin at that. Travis continued to sneer down at her. She was calm again, though, quiet again with that somehow graceful quietness. She regarded him steadily as the horse whickered and stepped too near her.

"I know you don't want to speak to me," she said finally. "But you must."

6

"Twilight and evening bell,
And after that the dark!"

The poet's words came back to Winter as he sat on a rocker on the hotel porch that night, as he gazed out over the railing at where the vast lake lay sunk in shadow. There was an actual bell tolling out there somewhere. A bell on a buoy, probably, the buoy swaying on the waves, the bell sending out a mournful sound like the sound of the poem. And wasn't it the same poet who wrote,

"Ring out, wild bells, to the wild sky,
The flying cloud, the frosty light . . ."

Because there was a wild sky out there also, complete with flying clouds racing through the frosty light of the nearly full moon.

Lord Tennyson might have written the hour into existence.

Winter nursed his sorrow and a bourbon, weary of one and wary of the other. He wasn't looking for oblivion, just for understanding and a little peace. He thought back to his first session with Margaret Whitaker a few days ago. The way the therapist had studied his hands. The intelligence in her pale green eyes had made him feel exposed somehow, the mask of his past stripped away. She had known, he thought, or she had guessed or suspected: the things he'd done, the death he'd left behind him, death by those very hands often enough, and sometimes by the hands of the evildoers because of him, which was even worse somehow.

He huddled in his warm shearling, sipped his drink, but just barely sipped it. He didn't want to rely on alcohol to balance his mood. He'd known too many men who'd gone down that hole, who'd been dragged down it, a smiling devil clutching their throats.

And it would take a lot more than one bourbon to scrub that video of Jennifer Dean from his mind, to erase those words: *I wanted you to see. I wanted you to understand who it was that Travis Blake stabbed to death.*

He could almost—almost but not quite—bring himself to a sense—an emotional sense—of how it might have happened. He could almost—almost but not quite—graft his own soul-burdening experiences onto what he knew of Travis and create for himself the image of a man who would take a life like Jennifer Dean's. Travis, the Silver Star soldier home from the wars: what had he done but serve his country under fire? And what had he gotten in return from God: parents ruined, a sister gone off the rails, a wife self-murdered, a child he adored but didn't know how to raise. You can't come back to the country you fought for. You can't come back to the life you left behind.

Travis Blake had made Jennifer wait when she came to see him. He had made her trail after him as he took Midnight to the stables. She couldn't have liked it, him on the horse, her walking behind, walking fast to keep up, as fast as she could with her heels sinking into the snow and the damp earth. But she wasn't going to be left out there either, lost in the fog alone.

He made her wait while he brushed the horse down and put its blanket on and set it to its feed. He didn't say a word to her as he walked to the house, and he let her know through sheer attitude that he didn't want to hear a word from her either. Again, she followed him, though it seemed to make no difference to him whether she followed him or not.

He was a dark man, Travis, inside and out. Shaggy black hair and a black beard. His eyes seemed cruel. Icy pale eyes, they seemed brutal by the look of them, though Jennifer told Mrs. Atwater that she did not believe that, she did not believe in the brutality. He loved the child at least, Jennifer said. Jennifer had seen that in the way she had of seeing such things. She had seen his paternal love—the results of his paternal love—in the daughter's bearing. For all little Lila's shyness, there was something solid and confident about her. With no mother around, only a father's love could have supplied that.

All the same, they really did seem like cruel eyes at first glance. And he was big too, Travis was, well over six feet. Broad-shouldered and muscular and aggressive in motion. She was afraid of him—she said as much to Mrs. Atwater later. He was the sort of man any woman would be afraid of, unless she was drunk or a damned fool.

She followed him into the house. Caught a glimpse of the pitifully neglected interior. Old, stained, torn furniture wherever there was furniture, wherever

Travis's parents had left some furniture behind. Dust on the windows, dust balls on the floor in the corners.

Then they were through the living room, and he was at the kitchen sink, drawing himself a tumbler of water from the tap, downing the full tumbler without offering her anything, without saying anything to her. And she, with that inner stillness she had, did not try to break the uncomfortable silence, but waited through it, waited him out.

He banged the glass down on the counter. Turned to her with those pale, frightening eyes.

"Well?" he said.

"Your daughter is gifted. You must know that."

"So? Teach her. You're a teacher, aren't you?"

"I'm the librarian."

"Oh, right. You said in your message. Well, give her books to read, then. She likes books."

He drew more water into the tumbler and as he did, she said: "No. You cannot raise a child like that, Mr. Blake. Like this."

She did not even bother to gesture at the house when she said it. She was sure he understood her. And he did. He cocked one eyebrow at her, and nearly smiled, if a smile is what you'd call it.

"Is that right?" he said.

"You know it is, Mr. Blake. It's part of what's troubling you. Why you ride like you do."

"Oh yeah? How's that?"

"Like you do. We all see you on the hills. Like you're chasing some demon, or some demon's chasing you."

He may have tried not to laugh, but he did laugh. At her audacity probably. It wasn't a very nice sound, but better than some others she could have imagined.

"I know you love Lila very much," she said.

"Oh, do you?"

"Yes."

"What are you—Russian?"

"What? What does that matter?"

"I killed a Russian once. Crept up behind him and snapped his neck with my bare hands."

She flushed hot and scarlet. "Would you like me to turn around?"

He laughed again—another harsh laugh. But his eyes seemed to lighten. And she saw with some satisfaction that she had been right. His eyes weren't cruel, not really brutal, just sullen, just hurt and angry, like a boy's.

She was not afraid of him anymore, dead Russians notwithstanding. She took a step toward him to let him know. She rested her hand on the kitchen counter.

"Your love is the essential thing, the air she breathes, her meat and drink."

He turned away from her and stared down into the drain. He planted his hands on the sink rim, lifted his shoulders around his neck like fortress walls. "Well, she's all set up, then, isn't she?" he muttered.

"No. Of course not. This darkness you surround her with, your darkness, and this indifference to the ordinary ornaments of daily life—it's as if she has food and drink and air but no sunlight. She can live but she can't thrive. She can't begin to grow into her remarkable abilities."

He went on staring into the sink. He didn't answer her. And then, by a visible act of will, he did. "Her mother had a skill for that," he said. "The ordinary ornaments of daily life."

"Of course. I understand. It's a womanly skill. All the same, I wager if I went to Lila's room right now, I would find a duvet on the bed, and pretty pillows, and a doll and pictures on the wall . . ."

He faced her with a start of surprise so violent it was almost comic, as if she had told him the exact amount of money he had in his wallet or what he'd eaten for dinner this day two years before.

"You see, you do know," she said. "You understand what I'm saying to you."

Jennifer later told Mrs. Atwater that it was a testimony to his love for the child that he allowed this, allowed himself to be vanquished by her. It was not, as Mrs. Atwater supposed, because of the spiritual force of her—of Jennifer's—personality. If she had only had that to rely on, Jennifer said with a laugh, she might have left like his last Russian, carrying her head under her arm.

Instead, he turned again, hulked over the sink again, his shoulders for fortress walls. Then the walls came down like Jericho. He sighed. "Believe me, I've tried," he said softly. "I just can't."

"Yes," said Jennifer Dean. "You can. That is exactly what I came to tell you. If I didn't think it was so, I would not have come."

One more time, he looked at her, shaking his head now, his lips parted, gazing at her almost with wonder as if she had fallen from the heavens—which, as Mrs. Atwater said, was exactly what she sometimes seemed to have done.

He was still gazing at her like that when she turned away and walked out of the kitchen. He may have still been standing there, listening to her footsteps, as she passed through the empty living room, through the dusty grand foyer, and out again into the fog.

7

The flying clouds were gone by the time the frosty night was over, but the mournful Tennyson bell was still tolling out on the water somewhere as Winter left his hotel that morning and walked to his SUV.

It was another brisk, sun-bright day. He drove from the lake to the center of town and cruised slowly down the main thoroughfare, peering out through the windshield. He could see shopkeepers opening their quaint storefronts, the windows draped with colored lights and Christmas pine. He could see shoppers lining up at the coffee counters. He could see men and women in overcoats hurrying up the stone stairs of the county office building and the courthouse. Both buildings were classical structures of confident small-town majesty. Both seemed to have been built in the middle years of the last century.

And he came to the conclusion now: No, it wasn't just Victoria, it wasn't just what Victoria had told him about Sweet Haven. It was true: the military and ex-military presence was everywhere apparent here. There was a look many of the men had, a way of moving, a watchful confidence, and a look some of the women had too, that ladylike poise, that reckless scintillation in their eyes, the antic irony. Now in the early light, now that he was parked outside the courthouse, leaning against the door of his Jeep, watching the people pass, studying them, he could see it was all as Victoria had said. And he could see more . . .

At that moment, Victoria came out of the courthouse. She paused between the thick Doric columns at the top of the stairs. She stood searching for him long enough for him to think how lovely and wintry and cozy she looked in her wool coat and wool hat. Then she spotted him and smiled her hopeful high-school-girl smile and came down the stairs toward him.

He went around to the passenger side and opened the door for her. He caught the flowery scent of her as it mingled bracingly with the crisp air. He wished he hadn't caught the scent, but it was too late and there was nothing to be done.

"So what do you think of Sweet Haven?" she asked as the Jeep pulled away from the curb.

"It's nice. Lovely. It's like a Christmas card." When she didn't respond, he glanced at her and found her watching him narrowly. "What?" he asked.

"Well, I was about to say something like, 'I know you, Cameron Winter.' But that wouldn't be true, would it? I only thought I knew you once, but no one really does. But I do think I know you enough to know when you're not saying exactly what you mean. Or when you're not saying as much as you mean."

He smiled. They drove past the grand old Victorian houses just beyond the center of town. There were understated wreaths on their painted doors. There were trimmed pines laced with white fairy lights standing erect on their snowed-over lawns.

"I was thinking last night about something you said," he told her. "That you can't come back to the country you fought for. But you could here, couldn't you? Sort of. You could feel as if you had come back. Like you feel when you're looking at a Christmas card: that a sweet past has been frozen in place. That's what I meant about Sweet Haven. It's like a sweet past frozen in place."

She nodded. "Yes, I've thought about that too. It's what they meant to do, I'm sure of it. All these ex-soldiers. It has to be intentional. It's like a conspiracy of values. A conspiracy against decay. A plot against time."

As they got farther from the main road, the houses became more modest. As the houses became more modest, the Christmas displays became more elaborate. Some of the homes here were wholly outlined in blinking lights. Outside of one, a life-size Santa Claus climbed into a sleigh with a full complement of reindeer. "Merry Christmas" flashed boldly in the window of another—as if it were a tavern, Winter thought.

"Turn left up ahead there," said Victoria.

He guided the SUV into the parking lot of a nondescript apartment complex, three groups of two-story clapboard bungalows, neither elegant nor shabby. Winter stopped the car in the lot, but the pair of them continued to sit there for a moment, silent. They looked out at the buildings as if they were impressed to be here, as if the murdered woman's spirit sanctified the place.

"Did you search the records for her like I asked?" Winter said.

"I started the process. I have our assistant on it. Adam Kelly. He's good with things like that."

"It's kind of strange, isn't it? She comes out of nowhere. No one knows where she's from. There's no one to notify when she dies."

Victoria went on looking out at the bungalows. She murmured something in response—something like: "Mm. Yes."

"Didn't she have an ex of some kind?"

"Not that we could find."

"Still. You'd think the police would be able to find someone who cared about her, at least. Didn't the school do a fingerprint check when they hired her?"

Vic seemed to come back to herself from a long way off. She faced him as if just remembering he was there. "They did. Yes. She had all the certifications. A master's degree from State. No criminal record or anything like that."

"And no family."

"Apparently not."

Now it was his turn to sit far gone in thought. The sound of the Jeep door opening roused him. He turned and saw Victoria starting to climb out.

"What am I really looking for here?" he asked her.

That stopped her motion. She sank back into the seat. The cool air from outside blew over them through the open door.

"You said you wanted me to prove Travis was innocent," Winter said. "But that can't be right. It doesn't make any sense. He can't be totally innocent. Can he? With all the evidence against him. With his confession. What's your theory? That it's all some elaborate trick of some kind? A faked death or something?"

The sad little frown she gave him was downright pitiful, he thought. She looked like a little girl about to cry at being caught in a fib. "No," she said. "I thought of that. But it can't be."

"Right," said Winter. "Because all things being equal, he's going to go to prison for life. That's not much of a trick."

She sighed. "No."

"So what are we looking for exactly?"

It was a moment before she answered. It took her a moment, he thought, to come up with any answer at all.

"When you talked to the principal at the school—Mrs. Atwater—did she tell you about the little girl's birthday?"

Winter nodded. "She did."

"By all accounts, Travis and Jennifer were serious about each other after that. By all accounts, it was the real thing between them."

"I'm sure it was, but this wouldn't be the first time . . ." Winter began.

And she finished for him: ". . . a love affair ended in murder. No, obviously it wouldn't. And it's not like we don't have extenuating circumstances already. We do. The PSIR—the Presentence Investigation Report—talked about Travis's PTSD from the war. His wife's suicide. His emotional decline. It's easy to imagine how he could have gotten obsessed about something. Jennifer's secrecy. Some old boyfriend. It's easy to imagine how a man like him could have snapped. A moment of madness. There's room for mercy there. There is. He's charged with second-degree murder, so the judge has some leeway. We might be able to argue him down to twenty-five years instead of life. And if we could make the case that it was unintentional in some sense, we might even get the sentence down to fifteen."

"What sort of judge is he?"

"Judge Lee?" She made a vague gesture with her hand. "Former Army Ranger Lewis Lee? With the prosecutor weighing in—Former Army Ranger Jim Crawford?"

"So maybe they'll go easy on him as a brother in arms."

"Maybe," she said without much hope. "But these guys are straight arrow all the way. It's more likely they'll hold him to the high standards of the 75th Regiment and throw the book at him. That's what I'm afraid of anyway."

Winter nodded, considering. "So again, Vic, what are we looking for? It would help if I knew."

Victoria made a noise. "I don't know, I don't know. The whole thing just isn't right somehow. I just feel it." She pressed her fingers to her brow and massaged it as if she were in pain. Winter watched her. Her freckled cheeks bunched as she battled with her thoughts. He had always liked her freckled cheeks.

She sighed. She raised her face to him. "When my husband came back from Afghanistan, he wasn't the same. He was, I mean, but he wasn't. It was still him, for the most part, but in his eyes, there was something different. It's still different. I can still see it in there."

"Well, maybe that's just the way it is," Winter said. "Maybe it's not that you can't come back to the country you fought for, maybe it's just that you can't come back the same."

She didn't answer. She gazed out the windshield.

"And so—what?" he asked. "Travis Blake reminds you of Richard, so you want him to be innocent? You want me to prove your husband isn't going to kill you someday?"

"I don't know. I want it to make sense to me. Emotional sense," she said. "I mean, is it really possible that the man who came to that birthday party could be the same man who plunged a combat knife into a woman he loved, rolled her body up in a rug, and dumped it out in the middle of the lake?"

"Yes," Winter said at once. "In my experience, that's completely possible."

She glanced at him sidelong, petulant. "It's Roger, damn you. Not Richard. My husband's name is Roger."

"Roger, of course," said Winter drily, but she had already gotten out of the Jeep and slammed the door.

Winter lingered behind the wheel a moment. There was an image in his mind. It was the image of a dark man on a black horse, galloping across the ridges of the hills outside Sweet Haven. Like he was chasing some demon or some demon was chasing him. Of course he could have murdered her. Vic was just being sentimental, that's all.

The image of the rider faded, but Winter still sat there. He sat there until he realized it was only because Victoria's scent had lingered there with him.

Then, annoyed with himself, he pushed his way out of the Jeep into the chilly day.

He had to hurry along the apartment complex paths to catch up with her. Then she led the way into a bungalow in the middle of the group. He followed her up a flight of stairs to the apartment on the second floor. There was police tape on the door there, but Vic sliced through it with a metal nail file she had in her purse. She pushed the door open and let Winter go in first.

Jennifer Dean's apartment was exactly what he had been expecting. It was a tidy one bedroom almost completely devoid of any personal decoration. The framed sketches on the wall—forest scenes and lake scenes—they could have been pictures in a hotel room. The plates in the kitchen, the blankets on the bed, even the cosmetics in the bathroom—they could have been anyone's, purchased in a casual moment from the simplest online venue. Even the clothes in the closet and the dresser seemed to have been bought in the same casual way. The skirts, slacks, and blouses could have been picked out in half an hour from a department store website or two. Even the underwear was like that.

There were two exceptions to this general rule of anonymity. One: there was a Russian icon hung low on the wall near the bed, a picture of a gaunt

Madonna and a strangely adult child hand-painted on wood. Jennifer Dean probably gazed at them through the night shadows as she lay near sleep. And two: there was a book, one well-worn foreign paperback, on the bedside table. The librarian would be a reader, of course. But then where were the rest of her books? Winter imagined she read one at a time, threw each one away when she was done with it and got another, then read that, and so on.

He picked the book up and examined it more closely. It was in Russian.

"Dostoevsky," he said. "*The Brothers Karamazov.*"

Vic, who had been pawing through the clothes in the closet, turned to him, surprised. "How do you know that? You read Russian?"

He tossed the book back down on the bedside table. "It just smells like Dostoevsky," he said blandly.

He went to the bedroom window and peered out. He saw the snow on the grass. The road visible beyond a line of trees. It was a dull view—not unpleasant but vaguely depressing, if you were prone to depression, which of course he was these days. He thought of Jennifer here, alone, reading her Russian book, praying to her Russian Madonna, gazing out at the dull view as she fell in love with her American Silver Star hero.

The affair, as Victoria said, seemed to have begun at Lila's seventh birthday at the end of April. This was just two weeks after Jennifer had gone to see Travis at the Big House. There had been no party invitations sent out from the house, so Jennifer worried Lila's birthday would go unnoticed. She made sure the usual school party was a little more elaborate than usual. She served cupcakes in the library, and provided literary decorations: paper tablecloths, plates and cups bearing pictures of the heroines from Lila's favorite series of books. The children had a good, giddy time, smearing their faces with cake. Lila looked happy, flushed and smiling under her paper crown.

Lila had a special friend, Gwen. Gwen's mother—Hester Kelly was her name—had made a point of nurturing the relationship between the two girls because she saw that Lila needed it, with her mother dead, with her father lost in his own world of grief and anger. She, Hester, was also there to help out with the party. And the principal, Mrs. Atwater, dropped by for a while too.

All three women suddenly stood still, stunned, when Travis Blake walked through the door. After a moment of staring, Mrs. Atwater turned to Jennifer and beamed. It was her way of saying: *This was all your doing.* Which it obviously was.

Travis had cleaned himself up since the day he and Jennifer had met. He had trimmed his beard to a close scruff. Pressed his jeans. Put on a jacket and a clean shirt. He had even dialed down the fury in his eyes—or maybe it had simply faded on its own. Either way, he came into the school library more or less smiling and carrying a few presents under his arm.

Lila saw him from her seat at the head of the table. She gave a great, loud gasp of surprise, her mouth an *O*. As Jennifer and Hester stood side by side looking on, the child leapt from her chair and rushed across the room like a little gust of wind. She hurled herself against her father, clutching his legs, crying out, "Daddy!" with an unchecked fervor of gratitude and delight.

Jennifer went on watching in that quiet way she had, her body erect and unmoving—but her eyes filled. She had to take a slow, deep breath to keep from making a noise like a sob. Hester Kelly actually turned away, swiping quickly at her cheek with one palm. Then she clutched Jennifer's elbow and gave her a fierce look of triumph, a tribute to Jennifer's accomplishment.

But it was, Jennifer still insisted later, a token really to the father's love for the child: that he would wrestle down the beast of his dysfunction, set aside his rage, set aside even his male pride in order to surrender his private darkness to the will of an impertinent school librarian.

The end of the party was the end of the school day. Lila went out the door holding her father's hand and chattering as no one had ever heard her chatter before—chattering just like a seven-year-old girl who had had a birthday party and wanted to talk about it forever.

"Well!" said Mrs. Atwater to Jennifer. It was by way of congratulations.

Travis and Lila were out of sight around the corner—the little girl's gabble was still trailing back to where the three women stood in the library—when Jennifer noticed they had forgotten the pink wristwatch Gwen had given Lila as a present.

"Oh," she said. She darted forward and scooped the watch up and hurried out the door.

She called out as she ran after them—called out to the child, not the father. She was shy about calling out to the father for some reason.

"Lila!"

Both child and father turned and waited. Jennifer bent to deliver the watch into Lila's little hand. "You forgot this, sweetheart."

Travis looked on silently as his daughter received the gift. Jennifer was already walking back to the library before he called out to her.

"We're going roller-skating in Cadillac Park on Saturday," Travis said. He didn't call her name—he must have been shy too—and it was a moment before Jennifer registered that he was speaking to her. Then she turned, and he said again: "We're going to go skating on Saturday. Do you want to come?"

Still holding the wristwatch, Lila clutched her hands together and bounced eagerly on her toes, praying to the librarian to please-please-please come.

"Oh, I'm so sorry," Jennifer said. "I really can't. Another time maybe."

"She was hiding," Winter said now, turning from the window to where Victoria stood at the closet. "Someone was after her. The old boyfriend maybe. She was on the run. She must have been."

Victoria blinked as if she couldn't imagine it. "Really? Do you think? That seems so—I don't know—melodramatic. Doesn't it?"

"This empty room," Winter said. "No trace of anything personal. The one book. The way she never answered questions. And why did she refuse him—Travis—why did she refuse Travis when he asked her to go out skating with them after the birthday party?"

"But she did go. She showed up. Just like he did at the party. A surprise."

"Because she was drawn to him. To both of them. It overcame her fear."

"Do you really think . . . ?"

But then her phone buzzed in her jacket pocket. She brought it out and looked at it. "My assistant—Adam," she said, and answered, walking out of the room.

Winter heard her fading murmur as she moved into the living room. He looked down at the bed. He found himself imagining Victoria there. He remembered the feeling of her body against his.

He made a face. This was getting absurd, maudlin. He didn't really want her back in his life. It was just his sorrow. Just his loneliness. He was looking for some Christmas comfort, that's all. Passionate as they had been in their illicit couplings back in her school days, he had never really loved her. She had said as much when she left him. She was the one who broke it off, and she said to him: "I can't compete with the woman in your head, Cam. I don't even know if she's real."

He became aware of a presence and turned and saw Vic leaning in the bedroom doorway. Her usually animated face was slack with confusion. She was staring at the bed as if she also saw the two of them there, just as he did.

She noticed him looking at her. She lifted her eyes.

"What did he say?" Winter asked her. "Your assistant. What did he say?"

"He couldn't find any trace of her. Just like the police. No phone for her LKA. Nothing. So he contacted State."

"The school. The university. Where she got her masters."

"They had no record of her. So he contacted Williams where she got her BA."

"No record," said Winter.

"It doesn't make any sense," said Vic. "Her fingerprint check—her security check at the school—it turned up records in the computers, so how could the schools have nothing on file?" For a second, her gaze drifted and she stared at something invisible in the middle distance. Then, as if coming back to herself, she looked at him again. She said, "What does it mean, Cam?"

"It means there is no Jennifer Dean," Winter said. "There never was."

PART TWO

HEARTS IN SPACE

After that first time, I spent Christmas at Mia's every year. I spent Christmas with Charlotte, that is to say—that's the way I thought about it.

It was always the same. The same corny music. "Silent Night." "Deck the Halls." Albert and me going out to get the tree. Stringing up the lights in the front room. Building the train set. Setting up the little Christmas town with the locomotive going through it. Building the fire—I was always especially proud when I made the fire.

We always went to church on Christmas Eve. I even got a bit mystic and religious for a year or two, at least around December. That drove my mother crazy. What would her friends say? Then there were those unbelievable pastries Mia and her sister and Charlotte made. The smell of the food filling the house and the warmth of the oven filling the house. Those would have made a believer out of anyone. Albert's ghost stories by the fire. The smell of his pipe. Charlotte gazing up at him in adoration.

It was all the same every year. And that's how I liked it. I never wanted it to be different, not even a little bit. It's funny. When you're young, you always want things to change. You want to grow up. You want to go to new places, do new things. But in the end, it's the things like Christmas, the things that are always the same, that you love the most.

Although, of course, there was one thing about my Christmases that did change, I guess. Namely the people—us. Especially us children. I grew. Charlotte grew. Year by year. It would be impossible to describe how beautiful she became.

I had been in love with her from the beginning. Me seven, she nine. Me effectively motherless, and she this serious little housewife with her Teutonic blond braids and those depths of maternal tenderness in her blue eyes. I would see her from time to time throughout the year. She'd come to our place with Mia or I'd stay overnight at Mia's house. And then at Christmas, we'd have that extended time together. A week at least, sometimes two. But the fact is: she was always with me. In my mind, I mean. She was my dream girl from the first day I saw her. It was as if she was hovering over me, watching me, even when we were apart. If I was brave in some way—if I fought the school bullies or took wild leaps on my bike or tried to be a hero on the baseball diamond—whatever I did—it was all to impress that invisible, floating spirit of Charlotte. "The eternal feminine leads us on."

I don't remember exactly when the new element entered into our relationship, when my schoolboy crush became something more than that. I do remember this excruciating period—absolutely excruciating—when I was maybe twelve or thirteen and she was fourteen or fifteen or so. She was becoming a young woman at that point. Still prim and precise, still quietly witty and teasing and maternal but not a child imitating a woman anymore, a woman in fact. And if she had been one of Mia's porcelain figurines when she was a child, now she was an angel in the flesh. I swear, if I hadn't had her right there in front of me, if I had had to invent her, I would have invented her exactly as she was. She was like Christmas itself: I wouldn't have changed a thing.

But I'm drifting away from my point. My point is: she was a young woman while I was still a boy. Only then, one day, I wasn't quite a boy anymore either. I mean, I was, but I had that first charge of manhood going through me, that first urgent fire.

Well, it was a perfect formula for unrequited misery. Because you see, she still saw me as the little boy she had sat with that first Christmas after the ghost story scared me. She still saw me as the child who licked the batter from the bowl after she was finished laying the Christmas cookies out on their pan. She would still give me the batter bowl, in fact. And I would still take it—I love cookie batter. And I would scoop the batter out with the wooden spoon and she would watch me sidelong as I licked the spoon clean and she would smile to herself like a woman smiles watching a child. But all the while now—all the while I was scooping out the batter—I was imagining what it would be like to take her in my arms, to press her close to me, to kiss her like they kissed on television, all that mysterious business with the mouths and tongues and hands I hadn't quite figured out yet from a mechanical point of view.

And she would say things to me like, "Now you are so big, sweet . . ." She didn't have a German accent, but she had this German way of phrasing things that was uniquely hers. My whole heart leapt at the sound of it. And she would say things like, "Now you are so big, sweet, but I remember when you fell down on the pebbles and hurt your knee that time and I had to read to you for half an hour before you stopped crying. Do you remember that?" Oh God, it was agony. There I was, wondering what it would feel like to reach out and touch her sweater where it swelled over her breast—and in her mind, I was still seven years old. "Do you remember, sweet?"

Then came the year I was fifteen, the Christmas I was fifteen . . . Things have happened to me in my life, hard things, painful things. I've been shot. I've been stabbed. I could show you the scars, still there, still ugly. I've been left for dead on the street of a foreign city with no friend to find me and no way home. But nothing—nothing has ever been as painful to me as that Christmas.

Because she had a boyfriend, you see. Well, of course she did, right? She was seventeen. She was this lithe Kraut fairy from a Grimm fairy tale, eye-scorchingly lovely. The boys must have been lined up to get at her. So of course she chose one of them. What girl wouldn't?

Michael was his name. This is more than twenty years ago, but I've never forgotten him. I can still see him as if he were standing in front of me. Tall and gangly with a long, horsey face, but not unhandsome. Polite. Smart. Full of boy confidence. He was on the football team, I think. Almost every night that Christmas season, she went out with him to a dance or a party. And I would have to sit at home like a child with Mia and Klara and Albert. I'd have to sit on the couch with them watching musical cartoon Christmas shows on television. Frosty's Winter Wonderland *or some such crap. All the while wondering: What were they doing? Michael and Charlotte. Was she kissing him? Was he touching her the way I wanted to touch her? I tried to convince myself she wouldn't do that. Not my Charlotte. She wasn't the sort of cheap floozy who'd let a boy touch her just because he was smart, polite, handsome, and a football hero and she was seventeen! What a pitiable little idiot I was.*

Sometimes the two of them—the two young lovers—would stay out late. I would have to go to bed. I would lie awake as I did that first Christmas. Only now, it was like having knives driven into me, like lying on a bed of knives with the homunculus of my jealousy sitting on my chest, pressing me down onto the blades. I prayed to Jesus that Michael would be run over by a car. That was my special Christmas prayer. Hit Michael with a car, Lord, please. I didn't want him to die, not exactly. I daydreamed that he'd be run over, but I'd revive him with CPR. Or I'd risk my life to push him out of harm's way at the last minute. Then I'd turn to see the dawning realization in Charlotte's eyes, you know. That it was really me she loved. That she knew I was not a little boy anymore. I was at long last her hero.

I had a whole year to think about that miserable Christmas. Fifteen to sixteen. That was the year I lost my virginity. Tess Hutchinson. The girls apparently had a bet to see which one of them could bed me first. As if any one of them couldn't have bedded me. They only had to ask. Tess was the one who asked. She was a beauty too. But I literally had my eyes closed with her half the time because I was pretending I was with Charlotte. Still, at least the mystery was solved now. At least I knew—I had a full sense finally—of what it was I wanted.

So now, as winter came, as Christmas neared, I made a resolution. I simply couldn't stand this torment anymore. Could not stand it. So I resolved: this Christmas, when I saw Charlotte, when I had a moment alone with her, I was going to kiss her.

It was now or never. This was Charlotte's last Christmas at home before she went away to college. She wasn't going far away, but all the same, she was going to enter another world and I understood that. There would be a whole college society she had never experienced before. There would be college men. Michael was out of the picture now, that had ended, but there would be new, sophisticated college men. And I reckoned it this way: When I was thirteen and she was fifteen, I was a boy still, and she was becoming a woman. I could well remember how humiliating that had been. And I knew if I waited, she would go to college and it would be like that again. By the time I was seventeen, she would be in this new, adult college world, far beyond me. So if I was going to declare my love for her, it had to be now. And sure, it was a desperate gambit, but what did I have to lose? I had to do something. I couldn't stand the pain of loving her, not like this.

As you can imagine, this plan of mine was all I thought about. From the moment I arrived at Mia's house for my annual Christmas visit, I began looking for my opportunity. So obsessed was I with stealing this kiss that I didn't even notice how distracted and troubled Charlotte was that year. She was always a serious little person but always tender and witty too. This year, though, she seemed heavy with some secret sorrow. Once, when I entered her room unannounced, she quickly hid the book she was reading. I did not see the title, only a flash of the image on the cover: a field of black, red, and yellow stripes with something like a compass in the middle. I realized only much later it was the flag of East Germany. It was only much later that I understood: she was coming to terms with the truth about her homeland, the dictatorship where the citizens were terrorized by the secret police, the Stasi, and their hundreds of thousands of informers. Questions—unbearable questions she had until now managed to suppress—were beginning to shape themselves in her mind.

But at the time, her feelings and her troubles could not even begin to penetrate my armor of teenage narcissism. I thought nothing of the book she was reading, or of her troubled silences. I thought only of how and when and whether I would steal that kiss.

I got my chance almost by accident. An accident followed by a moment of inspiration. If it hadn't come to me like that, I don't know whether I would have ever found the nerve.

Charlotte and I had gone out to a mall to do some last-minute shopping. That is, she said she was going out to the mall, and I said I would go with her, hoping I'd find an opening for my desperate play.

It was awkward because I didn't have my driver's license yet, so she drove and I sat beside her, which made her the little mother and me the little boy again. I had to remind myself I was grown now and much taller than she was. Plus, I had made my resolution. I was committed. I was watching for an opening.

As we were driving home, a baker's truck passed us. It had the bakery's name written on the side: Geneva Bakery.

Charlotte glanced at it as it passed. And she said to me, "Did you know we used to live there? In Geneva?"

And I said, "No. Did you?" Geneva was only a couple of towns down the road, but I had never been there.

Charlotte said, "Yes. When first we came to America, we rented a little house there. Just for about six months before my father got his job and we could afford to move where we are now. I don't remember it at all. I was just a baby. But Father has shown me photographs."

That's when I had my inspiration. I said, "Well, we should go there. Do you know where the house is? We should go and look at it. It would be fun." I was thinking, you know: This might be my moment. If we went to Geneva, if we got out of the car—if we were standing together—looking at her old house and feeling Christmasy and nostalgic—maybe standing someplace away from the road—somewhere Mia or Albert or Klara or anyone who knew us would never see us—I might have the courage then. I might take the chance.

I could tell Charlotte liked the idea. "You know, I haven't been to see it in so many years," she said. "I almost forgot about it." She glanced at her watch to see if we had time. She said, "It's only twenty minutes away. I know where the house is."

I egged her on: "Let's go!"

And she said, "It would be fun to see it."

Just then, the bakery truck turned off onto the highway ramp in front of us. As if on impulse, Charlotte swung the wheel and we followed.

Well, my heart was suddenly pounding in my chest. Between providence and my quick wit, I had engineered an opportunity. All I needed now was the courage.

There was a light snow falling as we came into Geneva. A patina of white already covered the lawns. Charlotte pulled the car to the curb in front of a shabby little clapboard cottage at the end of a dead-end street at the far edge of town. The house barely looked large enough to hold a single person let alone a family. A lonely string of colored lights was hung sloppily along the edge of its tar-paper roof. The snow lay prettily on a postage stamp of grass and on the few pieces of cheap lawn furniture scattered around it. Behind the house, I could see a scraggly winter wood on a plunging slope. I don't imagine it was much to look at normally, but with the snow decorating the branches, it had at least a touch of holiday romance.

"Oh, look at it," said Charlotte tenderly to herself. And the tone of her voice gave me hope. This was the sort of mood I wanted her in.

I got out of the car, reckoning she'd follow. And she did follow. And we stood shoulder to shoulder, our hands in the pockets of our winter coats, staring at the place.

I said, "I don't know how you all managed to fit in there. You and your father and Mia and Klara."

She shook her head.

The house was dark inside. It seemed empty. And there was no traffic on the road. I might have made my move right then and there, but I had this instinct that I should get Charlotte out of plain sight. So I wandered away and strolled to the back of the house as if to get another view. I came to the edge of the little forest there and stood just where the land sloped away behind me.

Charlotte, of course, came to join me. She was incredibly fetching. Her cheeks were pink with cold, and she had an adorable green felt beret tilted jauntily over her braids. Again, we stood together, her shoulder touching mine. We were both silent for a long moment. My heart was beating so hard I thought it was going to explode. I felt as if everything I wanted in the world depended on the next second. I guess it did.

I asked her finally, "What are you thinking?"

And she said, "I am sad a little, you know. To go away to school next year. To leave my family. My father. I am excited. But I am sad also sometimes."

And I said, "Charlotte," in such a tone that she naturally turned to me, wondering what it meant.

And I did it. I took her clumsily by the shoulders and leaned down and pressed my lips to hers.

She didn't kiss me back. Her mouth stayed closed. But she didn't pull away either. And though her body stiffened with surprise at first, a second later, I felt her relax in my grip. Another moment and her lips softened against mine, and my heart was flooded with her.

I felt her start to draw away, so I drew away. I scanned the depths of her eyes, desperate to know her reaction. The expression on her face has never left me. I can see it right now. There was a moment of surprise followed by understanding. Then her lips parted on a slight smile—a smile of kindness and of gentle pleasure—as she grasped the entire secret of my heart.

If she had rejected me then, it would have crushed me. If she had pitied me, I never would have recovered. But while what I saw in her eyes and in her face wasn't the reciprocal passion I hungered for, it was not an impossible barrier either. Her expression was saying to me: Not now, but maybe someday. *My love for her was wrong now—even I felt that, now that the moment of crisis had passed. I was too young. She was starting a new life. It wasn't our time. But that time might come. It might. It was possible. All of that was in her expression and in her eyes.*

She lifted her gloved hand and gently touched my cheek. "Oh, sweet," she said, and I caught her hand and pressed it against my face with a surge of gratitude.

I don't know what I would have said next, what either of us would have said. Because before either of us could speak, something happened. Something caught her eye. Her gaze shifted—shifted away from me to the trees behind me, to the slope behind me and down the slope.

And she said, "My God. Look at that."

As I turned around to see what was there, she was already moving past me, stepping to the edge of the descent. Then I saw what she saw—and I followed her.

There was a church at the bottom of the hill. I could see the shape of it through the light snow and through the branches of the winter trees. I recognized the place at once, just as she had. It was the church from Albert's story—from the ghost story he had told us that first year about the girl in the German city. He had described the building so clearly, with its square tower that became circular and then the conical brass steeple, green with verdigris, at the top. It was unmistakable. It was the church where the ghost's grave had been, where the headstone was that held her name, Adelina Weber.

Charlotte glanced at me. "Do you see it?"

I nodded.

She said, "Come on, sweet."

She headed off down the hill. And I went after her.

I wasn't really thinking about what we would find. Mostly, I was glad of the distraction. I was glad to get out of that moment after our kiss. The expression on Charlotte's face had been such a gift to me, such a treasure. I did not want us to spoil it by trying to say what could not be spoken.

So down the hill we went, dodging the snowy trees as gravity gave us speed. We tumbled out of the woods, and in a few more steps we were at the iron fence around the old church. We looked over the railing into the graveyard beyond, just like Albert did in his ghost story.

"I guess this is where he got the idea for it," I said.

"Mm," was all Charlotte answered.

I thought she sounded troubled. When I glanced at her, I could not tell what was unfolding in her mind. It was something, though. Some revelation was coming to her as we stood there.

Then, serious, focused, determined, she moved to the little gate in the fence. She opened it. Went in among the graves. I followed her.

"What is it, Charlotte?" I said.

She didn't answer. She moved from monument to monument with a purpose, glancing at the names. She passed beneath a statue of a mourning angel, its cowled head bowed above her. She let her hand trail over a small stele. And then she stopped before a snowcapped stone at the head of a grave.

The snow came down harder as I moved up beside her. I glanced up at the dark shape of the church towering over us, and I felt a sour, hollow misgiving inside me, a haunting sense of the uncanny, as if we had actually stepped into that ghost story Charlotte's father had told us all those years ago.

I stood beside her. My gaze followed hers. We looked down at the gravestone. I half expected it would bear the name of Adelina Weber.

But instead, the name was Emilia Shaefer.

"What is it?" I said again. "Who is it?"

"It's my mother," Charlotte said softly, staring.

"Your mother?" I said. "I thought your mother died before you all came over."

"Yes," she said. "So did I. That's what my father always told me."

We looked at each other. I did not understand what was going through her mind, but I had some sense now that it was not a sudden matter. It was the last link in a long chain of reasoning, a confirmation, I mean, of some dreadful suspicion she had harbored for quite some time.

Her body straightened. Her eyes went cold.

But all she said was: "I have been lied to."

8

"We're almost out of time," Margaret Whitaker said.

She observed Cameron Winter closely. She had let him run on uninterrupted until then, and he had sunk into a kind of reverie as he told his story. His mind was in the past with Charlotte. He had to shake himself when Margaret spoke, as if she had awakened him from a dream.

Margaret stayed quiet while he returned to himself. For those few moments, she could see the face of the boy he once was. It was there like pentimento, a faint image just visible beneath the surface. She was aware of a sensation of maternal sympathy for the lonely child he'd been back then. It made her think of her own son, who lived lost and unfulfilled in a distant corner of the country. It was part of her job to be aware of such feelings in herself, to make sure they didn't distort her view of the client. Still, the wistful longing on Winter's face made her think of her own boy with regret.

"I'll have to finish this story another time," said Winter. "If I'm not boring you, that is."

She was too skilled to take that bait. Instead she said, "I'm curious. You said you'd been shot at some point. Stabbed. Why? You said you were once left for dead on the street of a foreign city. How did that happen to you?"

Margaret felt a twinge of low satisfaction to have caught him off guard. She watched, faintly amused, as he shifted uncomfortably in his chair.

"That's what you want to know about?" he said. "I tell you this whole story about my first love and that's what you want to ask me?"

"I think that's what you want to tell me about, Cameron. I think that's what you've been trying to tell me."

He made a face as if she were being absurd. "Really? That's what I want to tell you? Not about Charlotte?"

Margaret smiled. Even he knew he was dodging her now. "You're an English professor," she said. "You should appreciate the structural complexity of a narrative. You told me a story about a man who told you a story about a ghost, which was really a story about his dead wife. I assume her death haunted him in some way."

"Yes." Winter conceded the point. "Yes, it did."

"And that story you told me about a story that was really another story is itself another story that is really another story." She did her best to smile as if this were a joke between them.

But Winter did not smile. He said: "Another story about what?"

She made a small gesture and gave him a look of amused reproach that was more maternal than she meant it to be: like a patient mother who has caught her child in a mild deception. "That's what I'm asking you, Cameron. I imagine you're trying to tell me about something that haunts you. Aren't you? Something that weighs you down. Something that's making you . . . What's the word you used?"

"I'm sure you remember," said Winter sullenly.

"Yes, I do. Melancholy. It makes you melancholy. More each day, I think you said. So what is it? What's weighing on you? Why were you shot? Why were you knifed? Why were you left for dead on the street of a foreign city?"

"I thought you said we were almost out of time." Winter looked at his watch. "We are out of time. Past it."

"There's time for you to tell me, if you'd like to."

Cameron sighed. Margaret was struck again by his good looks, that face like the face of a Renaissance angel. She was struck, too, by how often in this sad life a person's gifts are useless in helping him fulfill his true desire. She had treated artists who wished they knew the trick of making money, and money men who had always wanted to be artists instead. And here was a man who was attractive and well-spoken and appealing and should have had no problem attracting a partner to share his life with, and yet he was stranded inside his loneliness, he could not find the love he had been looking for since he was a child.

"What if I don't want to tell you?" he asked, trying to laugh the whole thing off. "What if I don't want to tell you what you say I want to tell you?"

"Then I'll have no way of knowing," the therapist said.

He nodded in answer, nodded silently for a long time, smiling bitterly to himself. Then, staring down at the tan carpet, he spoke in a quiet, unemotional voice that somehow carried so much sorrow in it, it sent a pang clear through the center of her.

"I've killed people, Margaret," he said.

And before she could stop herself, she answered, "Yes, dear. I know."

9

Winter was still agitated from the therapy session when he walked into the shopping mall. Even so, he couldn't help but appreciate the comic scene that greeted him. Through the streams of shoppers passing the storefronts, he could see Stan "Stan-Stan" Stankowski standing just in front of Santa Claus. The Santa Claus was a life-size mechanical figure in the window of the department store behind him. Santa was positioned by a fireplace next to a Christmas tree. He was removing a present from his sack again and again. *Ho ho ho.* Stankowski, on the other hand, was a federal agent working undercover. He was positioned out in the cold. He didn't look happy about it. There were no *ho*s.

Like most undercover agents, Stan-Stan Stankowski was approximately one hundred percent out of his ever-loving mind. He approached each new case like a method actor approaching a role—which made sense, since his life and the imaginary TV show about his life that was always playing in his head were indistinguishable to him. In this exciting episode, he was infiltrating a motorcycle gang engaged in human trafficking. By way of preparation, he had beefed up his five-foot-seven frame considerably and had grown a bushy white beard. Standing there hunched with his hands jammed in the pockets of his leather jacket, his black watch cap pulled low over his bushy eyebrows, and an expression of unholy wrath blackening his acne-scarred face, he looked like Santa's evil twin.

Winter walked up beside him and pretended to be looking in the window. Stan-Stan pretended to be waiting for someone else.

"For a minute, I wasn't sure which bearded fat man was you," Winter said.

Stan-Stan snorted and muttered something decidedly out of keeping with the spirit of the season.

"What the hell do you want?" he said to the passing shoppers. "I thought you were an English teacher now or something." He had a voice like a tractor pull: a low rumble that threatened to become an explosion.

"I am an English teacher," Winter murmured at the animatronic Claus behind the windowpane. "I wanted to ask your opinion about the use of classical references in Keats's 'Hyperion' as compared to Shelley's *Prometheus Bound*."

"I'm risking my life and, what's worse, I'm freezing my ass off, and you're making stupid jokes."

Winter smirked. But Stan-Stan was right: it was hellish cold out here.

So he got down to business. "I'm doing a job for an attorney named Victoria Grossburger up in Sweet Haven," he said. "She's looking for background on a murder victim named—"

"Yeah. This is the Jennifer Dean case. I know."

"I figured this might be one of yours."

"It was always a mystery to me how a guy with a face like a ballerina managed to do so much figuring."

"Victoria's looking for background on the vic, and she's getting the runaround, or her assistant is. The police got the same runaround before her."

"Sad story."

"Whoever Dean was, she's dead now. What difference does it make if her info is released?"

"I don't know. It's not my end of things. I guess they're trying to protect trade secrets," said Stan-Stan.

"That doesn't make any sense."

"Well, yeah. They work for the government. You know what that's like."

Winter chuckled. The Santa Claus in the window laughed. He lifted a present out of his sack, but damned if it wasn't the same present as the last one he had lifted out. The guy was in a rut.

Winter glanced over his shoulder. Stan-Stan met the glance sidelong. His eyes were just as loopy as the rest of him, but there was a frantic spark of humor in there too.

"All right," he said. "I'll make a call. This what's-her-name . . ."

"Victoria Grossburger. She's the public defender. Her assistant's name is Adam Kelly."

"All right. From what I hear, this originates out of the West Coast. There's some sensitivities about it in-house, I'm not sure what. But I'll try to get her what I can get her."

"Thanks. And keep me out of it, would you."

"I'll pretend you don't exist. If nothing else, that'll help me sleep at night."

"I think you're the real Santa Claus, Stan-Stan."

Stan-Stan's response was not in the least Kringle-esque. A moment later, he had disappeared into the stream of shoppers.

10

Travis Blake's sister, May, lived in what Cameron Winter drily called "the Big City." It was only an hour and a half away from the capital, but it was also a world away.

Winter disliked the Big City intensely. Its skyscrapers flashed up above the water with a hollow glory, but its silver center emptied after dark. The workers scuttled home to hunkering neighborhoods on the outskirts. The majestic towers and innovative art houses and classical office buildings were left to look down each night on hunched homeless wandering the sidewalks mad like survivors of a cataclysm. In other neighborhoods, once fine, the wind whipped litter down broken pavements between unmown lawns and houses with their windows broken and their roofs caved in. The poor were mostly black here. The rest were so pale they were barely white, just sickly. The whole tenor of the town grated on him.

Winter drove toward the city under a slate-gray sky. There was snow predicted. He was still agitated about that therapy session—even more agitated now that he was alone in the car with his thoughts. He was haunted by the sound of his own voice when he'd confessed the truth to Margaret Whitaker. The plaintive childlike anguish of self-accusation. *I've killed people, Margaret.* Was that really all he had been trying to tell her? Not about Charlotte? Just about the dead? But no, it wasn't all the dead, was it? Just the one. The one killing for which he could not forgive himself.

He wished he had never gone to see Margaret Whitaker in the first place. He tried to put her and the whole therapeutic process out of his mind. He glanced at his phone where it lay on the passenger seat. Not that he wouldn't hear it ring through the SUV's media system, but he was impatient. He was eager to get word from Victoria, to learn what her assistant had found out about the real identity of Jennifer Dean. It shouldn't take him long, now that Stan-Stan Stankowski was helping out behind the scenes. If nothing else, the new information would change the subject in Winter's own mind.

It was only midday when he reached the city center, but the glowering sky made the air as dark as evening. That, in turn, made the elaborate Christmas light displays brighter, gaudier. On the square block around the central park, every tree was draped with flowing skirts of blue or white illumination. The outglow shone on drab and broken storefronts brooding in the gray background.

He traveled on and reached May's house. To him, it seemed a miniature of the whole grim city. It was a craftsman cottage, once maybe lovely, but a ruin now. Green tips of the overgrown grass sprouted out of the thin covering of snow on the front yard. The porch roof was sagging. The white paint on the clapboards was chipped. The whole structure was beginning to crumble in on itself. The house on its right was an abandoned hovel of brick. The house on its left was barely visible behind the piles of trash scattered across the lawn. And yet once upon a time, this had been a neighborhood the middle class aspired to live in.

May's yard was littered with radical political signs. Their slogans rose above the snow cover angrily. There were signs and stickers in the windows too.

The windows were covered with lopsided shades ripped in strips, as if a cat had been at them. And there was the cat, in fact, a sleek gray one, sitting on the sill, staring out at him as he parked at the curb, watching him as he walked to the door.

He knocked and little sister May answered quickly, as if, like the cat, she had seen him coming. She was just as advertised. Small and hungry-thin and fragile. Her naturally sweet face seemed to Winter to have been brutalized by those famous piercings of hers: a steel stud in the side of her nose, steel rings up the edge of her ear, and a steel bead in her tongue that made him inwardly flinch for her. Her hair was clipped nearly to nothing, like a soldier's, on day one of basic training. And though her tattoos were mostly covered by her heavy sweater—because the house was almost as cold as the out-of-doors—Winter could see scrolls and tendrils of purple ink curling up from under the collar.

But if the girl was a walking red flag of rebellion against her bourgeois upbringing, she was not rude or sullen. She greeted him with a friendly smile and ushered him politely into a dark, unkempt, and cluttered living room of third-hand furnishings. She gestured him to an exhausted-looking green sofa. Like any good hostess, she asked him whether he'd like a cup of tea. He said yes, and she disappeared into the kitchen.

While he waited for her, he gazed out the window at the backyard. There, to his surprise, was Lila, Travis's little girl. She was playing in the shallow snow with a reedy, effeminate-looking black man in his twenties. They were lying on their stomachs face-to-face, building an army of tiny snowmen between them. They talked amiably as they worked. They both seemed happy or at least serene.

"That's Jed," said May. She had returned with two mugs of tea. She was looking out the window and smiling. "He and Lila are crazy about each other." She set the tea on the chipped coffee table before him.

"She seems happy," said Winter.

"Yeah. Kids are resilient, aren't they? We thought she might have trouble sleeping or something. From all the trauma, you know. But she's been fine." When he nodded without answering, she said, "I don't think you should talk to her, though. Like I said on the phone, I don't want her questioned about it. She wasn't there that night anyway. She was at a friend's house."

"Of course. That's fine. I'm sure you can tell me anything I need to know."

She settled across from him in an old easy chair. It was covered with a blanket to hide the tears in its fabric. They both sipped their tea and watched the child playing for a few moments.

"Will she be staying here with you?" he asked her.

She pursed her lips—sadly, he thought—and shook her head. "Her godfather's going to come and take her in a few days. That's Travis's choice. Which makes sense. He's a military guy. An ex-Ranger. Straight. Married with two kids. More in keeping with Travis's values. Also he's in business. He's got money. I couldn't really afford to give Lila what she needs."

Winter went on watching the child in the backyard for a few seconds more. He was considering May's words—*kids are resilient*—turning them over in his mind like a jeweler turning a gem in the light to see if it was real or paste.

He became aware that May was studying him. As he shifted his eyes to her, she said: "So your thing is—what? You're trying to find, like, extenuating circumstances?"

"For lack of a better term, yes. Something to give the sentencing judge an excuse to show some mercy."

May frowned thoughtfully into her tea. "Do you think Travis deserves mercy?"

"I don't know. His lawyer thinks so. But he's your brother. What do you think?"

There was a pause while she drank, looking down at the worn carpet. He thought she looked very young, very fragile. Like a child playing grown-up. He drank too. She finished first and gave a soft "ah." She said: "Maybe. Some mercy. It's not all his fault. He is what they made him."

"A soldier, you mean?"

"A man. I meant a man but, sure, a soldier too. Same kind of thing. He lived out what he was taught, didn't he? Love equals possession. Love equals domination. The violence is built in. It's the culture."

All this struck him as rote, memorized second-hand philosophy. He was impatient to get past it. "It doesn't surprise you, then?" he asked her. "That he would do what he did?"

"Why would it surprise me? It's the culture, like I said."

"Not everyone in the culture stabs his lover to death."

She shrugged, avoiding his eyes.

"I guess I'm asking about your brother specifically," Winter said. "When you think about your brother as an individual—does what he did surprise you?"

She lifted her eyebrows almost to the edge of her crewcut as if it startled her to hear the question rephrased that way. He noticed for the first time that one of her eyebrows was also pierced. There was a small steel bead at the base of it. Like the bead in her tongue, it made him think about what she had done to herself.

For a moment, she gazed at nothing through the steam rising from her mug. The room was not well lit, and it was difficult for Winter to study her face, but he tried.

The sound of Lila's little-girl laughter reached him from outdoors. He realized suddenly that he liked May. He felt for her. She was like her house, he thought. Hidden behind slogans and bumper-sticker thought formulas. Broken and neglected like the house, but once fine. He taught at a college, after all; a pierced tongue and tattoos and defiant cant was not a disguise that could hide much from him. He suspected he was looking at a young girl in terrible emotional pain, too much pain for her to come out into life and engage with its complexities. But he liked her heart, he thought. His instinct told him her heart was kind.

"I have to admit, I really did think he loved her," she said finally. "So I guess what happened surprised me in that sense. I mean, you talk to Jean . . . My partner, Jean. When I talk to Jean, she says it's all inevitable. It's just the way we live in this culture. It's the capitalism. That's what Jean says. It transforms people into property, so love becomes ownership and domination and then . . . Well, in every act of love, the murder is implied. Isn't it?" She looked up at him—expectantly, he thought. She was hoping he'd confirm all this rhetoric for her. When he didn't confirm it, when he only waited, she was left with his question again: What about Travis Blake as an individual? Finally she murmured, "But when you bring up Trav personally . . ."

And then there it was. The very pain he had been thinking of a moment before: there it was suddenly naked on her face. It turned her pale eyes glassy for a second. It was so intense, it was hard for him to look at it.

"No!" she said—softly, as if she didn't want the house to overhear. "No, that wasn't like Travis at all. I mean, he was old-fashioned. Traditional. He wanted things to be the way he thought they were supposed to be. You know? The way they were at home, when we were growing up, before he left, before it all unraveled. But he wasn't a—a brutal person. Not with me. And not with her, definitely. Not with Jennifer, I mean."

"You knew her? You saw them together?"

She nodded but not to him, to something in the air, rather, something he couldn't see. "Jennifer would bring them to visit. She would bring them both, both Travis and Lila. She wanted me to be able to see them. So she—" May gestured toward the child in the backyard. "So Lila would have a chance to get to know me. You know, because I'm her aunt. Patricia—Lila's mother, Travis's wife—she never would have done that. She never would have thought of something like that. And Travis would never have thought of it on his own, especially after Patricia died and he got so screwed up, shut himself off from everything. But Jennifer—Jennifer made sure they came to visit. Sometimes she brought just Lila. And sometimes Travis and Lila would come on their own too, just the two of them, even when Jennifer wasn't around. But it was because of Jennifer. That's why they came."

"Jennifer sounds like she was a special person," Winter said.

"She was!" That first reaction seemed to break from May before she had the chance to stop it. Then she backtracked. "Well, you know, she was very locked down, very committed to her traditional role. Totally on board with Trav's whole soldier-man, patriarch narrative. But still," she conceded, "if you look at it the way you were talking about before, if you look at her personally as an individual—I really liked her. I was really sorry about what happened. I was really sad about it."

Winter put on a sympathetic face. And, in fact, he was sympathetic. He could hear how much these family visits had meant to her. Because on the one hand, there was her philosophy—or her partner Jean's philosophy—with its simplistic explanations and its neat categories. And on the other hand, there was the reality of her inner world, the mess of it, a ruin like the city, abandoned by the people—by the culture, as she would say—that had made her what she was. Her mother and father had rejected her. Her brother had been lost to her, first at war, then in that galloping midnight darkness of his. And now he—both he and Jennifer—were gone completely, Jennifer dead, Travis in jail. And here May remained, thought Winter, all alone. And he felt for her. Because he was alone. Because it seemed to him just now that we were all alone in the end: hearts in space, drifting far and away from the impossible planet of the past.

"And you said he loved her," Winter said. "You said Travis loved Jennifer."

Staring at nothing, May nodded vaguely.

"Did that change at some point?" he asked.

She went on nodding, but Winter wasn't sure she'd even heard the question.

But she had heard it. She said, "Yes. Yes, I think so. I think something did change. I know it did."

A burst of noise from the backyard distracted them both. They turned toward the window. Lila and the young man were on their feet now, playfully throwing handfuls of snow at each other. They were shouting and laughing hilariously.

Winter was the first to bring his attention back to the room. He watched May's profile as she went on gazing out the window. The haircut was like a sign of penance, he thought. The piercings were the act of a flagellant. The made-to-be-sweet face wore her inner agonies plainly once you knew to look for them. She was a young woman who had lost the creature comforts of her childhood, lost her parents' acceptance and love, and had now lost her brother and his lover who had started to bring the family back together.

As Winter considered her thin form—her hungry little form almost swallowed by the big sweater—because the house really was as cold inside as the outdoors—it suddenly occurred to him with full force: something was terribly wrong here, something about all this made no sense.

"Will you tell me?" he asked her. "Will you tell me about what changed between Travis and Jennifer—what brought him to murder her, I mean?"

She nodded again, vaguely again, as if she were far away or lost in a dream.

"I will," she said.

11

As soon as Winter climbed back into his SUV, he took the phone from the pocket of his shearling coat and checked it. Still no call from Victoria, no word about her investigation into the true identity of Jennifer Dean. He lay the phone on the passenger seat where he could see it at a glance.

As he started the engine, he looked up at the collapsing house with the political signs and stickers guarding it and the unmown grass-tips peeking through the snow. The cat and May were both watching him from the window now. The gray cat sat on the sill, and May stood behind it, holding the torn shade aside and peering out over the cat's head. Winter had the strange sense he was abandoning her. But to what? And how could he stay?

He slipped the Jeep into gear and drove off, eager to put the Big City behind him. He headed back to Sweet Haven.

As he drove, he thought of the story May had told him. He imagined the scenes, filling in the emotional blanks in that way he had.

The love affair between Travis Blake and the woman who called herself Jennifer Dean had stuttered to a sudden start like a match struck twice. It was as if it was so obvious to them they should be together that they silently agreed to dispense with the preliminaries.

That Saturday after the child's birthday party, Jennifer had surprised both Travis and Lila by joining them where Lila was roller-skating in the park. (This was the story as Travis had told it to his sister, and as Winter imagined it now.) Lila had been thrilled to see the librarian arrive. She had shouted from the skate park, "Watch me, Miss Dean, watch me!" as she rolled around the concrete oval under the April trees. Jennifer had watched over the skate park wall and Travis had watched too, standing beside her. And even at Lila's first trip around, Travis had slipped his hand into Jennifer's hand, and she had pressed his hand in greeting.

It was like that: a settled thing between them right away, an expected and accepted thing. Only later had there been that hesitation, that need to strike the match a second time even as it sparked and flared.

They had returned to the Big House, all three of them. They had all eaten pizza together in front of a fire in the grate. They had put Lila to bed, and Jennifer had read a story to her. Then Jennifer came out of the bedroom and said: "I'd better go."

They were at the door when Travis kissed her. Which probably would have been fine, he later told May. Which probably would have been nice, he said, a gentle good-night kiss. But something surged in him after so much loneliness, so much grief at the death of his wife and grief at everything. Because, like May, he had lost the family of his childhood and who knows how much more.

"There was the whole war thing," May told Winter. "He'd seen a lot of bad stuff. You know?"

Winter did know. Not only had Travis seen his friends torn to pieces by bullets and roadside bombs, but there was also that inexpressible loss of innocence that comes with killing. Winter hadn't even tried to explain that to May. He had never tried to explain it to anyone, for that matter, not even himself. But he understood why Travis had suddenly grown desperate during that first kiss, why he had pulled Jennifer to him too hard, and forced himself into her too deep so that she started to struggle in his hands and he held on one moment too long before he came to his senses and let her go.

Then she looked up at him, with wide eyes, dismayed. She shook her head—*no*. He was too appalled at himself even to apologize. He averted his eyes. Shaken, she turned and hurried away from him to her rattletrap Chevrolet. He stood in the doorway and watched her start the engine. She started it hard, so that it roared into the quiet of the spring night.

He pretended to himself that he wasn't devastated. But he was devastated. He had fouled up that kiss so badly he could never make it right. She would drive away, and everything would be stiff and awkward and broken between them when he saw her next. There was no chance it could ever be fully mended.

But the woman who called herself Jennifer Dean did not drive away, not at once. She sat there gripping the wheel and looking out the windshield, her jaw working as the engine ran.

Then she stopped the engine. She got out of the car. She came back to him where he stood in the doorway. She took his face in her hands and brought him to her so he could kiss her again, not hard this time, not desperately, but also not just a kiss good night. It was the deep, slow kiss he would have given her the first time if he had done what it had been in his heart to do.

"It was a do-over," he later told May. "She gave me a do-over."

When they were done, somehow it was all right between them. She smiled up at him then went back to the car again. He stood in the door and watched her drive away. Maybe he wasn't already in love with her that moment, but he knew he would be. He would be soon.

And, in fact, they were lovers before the next week passed. They were eager, childlike lovers all through the spring. They stole lunch hours when the child was at school, and nights when she slept over at her friend Gwen's house. Sometimes they even conspired with Gwen's mother, Hester, to steal an afternoon here or there. Then Jennifer would ride behind Travis on Midnight, and he would take her to the romantic ruin of a nineteenth-century orphanage in the back hills, and they would lay down a blanket in the abandoned tower there.

Travis told his sister, May, about all this too, though he told it in a halting, euphemistic way, trying to get at the essence of what had happened to him while avoiding the intimate details.

May translated his thoughts to Winter. Jennifer, she said, schooled Travis's emotions with her body. She taught him gentleness and patience again.

"Before you lose things, you don't really know you can lose them," May said. She was speaking from experience now, having lost her family and the world of her childhood. "And then you do lose them, and afterward, you're always afraid. I think Travis had just lost so much, you know, in the war and then with Patricia dying. I think a lot of that anger inside him was also fear. I think Jennifer used her body to teach him she was there, she was really there right in the moment, and the moment, you know, is all you get, and you have to take it or you have nothing. I think that's what it was about between them in bed, him learning that, more than anything else almost. That was what I got from how he told it anyway."

Winter had reached the highway as he considered these things. The slate-gray sky had grown darker as he drove. Now the predicted snow began. There was no wind to blow it slantwise, so it was drifting down through the dark air, tumbling, slow and beautiful. It gathered on the trees beyond the shoulder. And when he caught glimpses through the trees of the white swirl over the dark blue water, it soothed his soul somewhat. He felt the Big City begin to lose its grip on him, like a skeleton's fingers slipping off his arm.

He could not help but picture Travis and Jennifer in bed together. He could not help but see them, in his mind's eye, learning to be lovers. All this talk with his therapist about Charlotte had brought his loneliness home to him. He did not know if simple loneliness was the source of his melancholy, but he felt the loneliness severely nonetheless. And when he thought of Travis falling in love with Jennifer, he began to fall in love with her a little too, he began to be there, emotionally, in Travis's place, in Jennifer's arms.

It was not too much to say—not too romantic or idealistic to say—that Jennifer brought the Big House to life again that summer. Their love brought the house to life again.

"You could really see it in Lila especially," May told him. "It was really obvious. She went from being this serious little schoolmarm to being a total chatterbox. *Yada yada yada.*" She made a mouth of her hand and opened and closed it. "You couldn't shut her up. She wanted to tell you everything all the time. It was really sweet, really hilarious."

Jennifer began to decorate the house and clean the house and cook for Travis and Lila. May became sardonic as she described Travis's awestruck reverence for all this housewifery as if it were a wonderwork of some kind instead of just the sort of thing a woman might do because she didn't want to live—and didn't want the child to live—like some angry man-bear in an animal cave.

"She would put a vase of flowers on the dining room table, and Travis would sit and stare at it as if she had magicked it out of thin air," May said.

She was sardonic about Travis's reverence for these feminine gestures, but Winter wasn't. Winter had been living alone for a long time.

Did Travis ever begin to suspect that Jennifer was not who she said she was? Did he ever begin to suspect that there was no such person as Jennifer Dean at all? Winter did not want to ask May directly, because he wasn't sure of the truth yet himself. He didn't like the idea of adding to the pain of her losses by erasing this woman who had meant so much to her. But May came to the point on her own.

"She never told him anything about her past. That really bothered him," she said. "It didn't bother him at first, but after a while it did. She told him she'd been in a bad relationship and didn't want to talk about it. But she never told him about anything else either, about her childhood or anything that happened before she arrived in Sweet Haven. And it just got to him after a while. Because he didn't just want to be with her, he wanted to know her. And he had so much *he* wanted to tell *her.* He'd been so locked down so long, he wanted to pour his heart out to her."

And he did pour his heart out to her. He found he could not help himself. During their walks, during their rides together on Midnight, or when they lay together in the quiet after making love, he poured out all the bitterness that had poisoned him. He had gone to war to serve his country, and what had his country done? Once he got started on that subject, he couldn't stop. His gallery of villains was vast, all-inclusive, filled to standing room only with almost everyone. The politicians of every stripe and the bankers and the billionaires and the feckless journalists—all had betrayed him. Ruined the economy and bailed out their rich friends while small businesses like his father's horse farm were ruined. The stick-in-the-mud haters had rejected his sister. The radicals had corrupted her with rage and idiot theories. Oh, and what about his wife—this was the worst of it, this made him angrier than anything—his wife, his Patricia, who wanted nothing but to do good in the world and raise their child—why hadn't anyone, not one single person, noticed when the drugs got hold of her and began to slowly strangle her to death?

"Jennifer would let him rant on and on about it all," May told Winter. "She was a good listener. She was a great listener. But after a while, even he noticed it was all one way. Like I said, she never told him anything. It made him feel isolated, like she wouldn't let him get really close to her."

Isolated, Winter thought, guiding his Jeep over the snow-slick highway. Isolated—but not suspicious. Not at first.

Then came the day at the beach. That, said May, was when everything started to change.

It was the last day of summer, the last day before Jennifer had to return to work to get ready for the school year. It was warm even before the sun rose. They had gone down to the water at first light to beat the crowds. It was not just the three of them, not just Travis and Jennifer and Lila. Gwen came, too, and Hester, her mother, and Hester's husband, Steve. That in itself said something about the changes Jennifer had wrought. Travis could do this now, he could be in company and have friends. It also helped that Steve was an ex-Ranger. Well, of course he was, this was Sweet Haven. But it meant that he and Travis could leave a lot unsaid between them, which was how Travis liked it most of the time.

It was a good day. The children built sandcastles and chattered together. Travis and Jennifer clowned around in the water. Steve and Hester smiled at each other and held hands as they watched them. Every hour, more people arrived, until finally the sand was almost completely covered with blankets and the sun was almost completely blocked out by umbrellas.

Around noontime, Jennifer got up and pulled her slacks on over the bottom of her bathing suit. She said she was going to the restroom. It was set in a concrete bunker at the top of the beach near the parking lot. Travis lay on the blanket and watched her as she picked her way through the crowd. Steve said the sort of thing men say at these moments, something like, "You won the lottery, my man."

Travis nodded—he felt he had won the lottery. And if he felt anything else, suspected anything else, he didn't say, not then. He and Hester and Steve just lay in companionable quiet and watched the children playing down at the water's edge. Fifteen minutes passed. Twenty minutes. Twenty-five.

Travis said: "Where'd she get to?"

Hester said: "Maybe she got a phone call."

Travis lifted his chin to point at Jennifer's phone. It was lying on their blanket in a pile with the blouse and scarf she'd worn over her bathing suit. So she couldn't have gotten a call.

He got to his feet, dusting the beach sand off his hands. He slipped into his flip-flops. He pulled on a T-shirt. He pulled his black ball cap down low over his eyes.

"Watch Lila for me, will you?" he said.

"He wasn't worried or anything," May told Winter. "He just had that feeling you get when someone's been gone too long—like you just ought to check on them, you know."

It wasn't easy getting through the crowd. Sidling between the blankets, ducking under the umbrellas, it took him five minutes to reach the place where the reeds began to grow through the shallower sand. The beach throng thinned here near the concrete path that led to the parking lot. The walking became easier. Soon, he crested a small dune, and the restroom bunker came into view.

He took a few more steps toward the structure. Then a movement in the distance caught his eye. He looked beyond the bunker toward the parking lot.

There was Jennifer. Jennifer and a man.

They were at the lot's far curb, between a black SUV and a lamppost. Travis was still more than a hundred yards away from them. He couldn't see the man clearly. What he could see was that the man was big, tall, and thick and threatening. He was standing close to Jennifer. He was gripping her by her arms and leaning down over her as she recoiled from him. It was a violent gesture, but it was intimate too. She was recoiling from him not because he was a stranger, but because she knew him all too well.

Travis shed the flip-flops at once and began to run toward the two figures. Ideas were sparking in his mind like bursts of static on a bad connection. This must be the "bad relationship," he thought. This must be the man she didn't want to talk about, the man she had come to Sweet Haven to escape.

Travis went off the path and cut across the sand. The sand gave way beneath his feet. He had to struggle to gain speed.

Now he saw Jennifer break from the big man's grip with an angry twist of her body. She stumbled back a step, and the man came a half step after her.

The reeds were poking into Travis's soles, but he didn't care. He kept running. As he got closer, he could see Jennifer look up angrily at the man. He could see the man speaking to her through an ugly smile. He was threatening her, Travis thought. He could see now that the man was older, fifty at least. He had thinning red hair. His features seemed smeared and unfocused, as if there was something wrong with his face.

Travis got past the reeds. The sand was packed harder here, and he picked up speed. He had an urge to shout out so the man would back away. But he didn't shout out. He didn't want to warn the man he was coming. He didn't want to scare the man off. He wanted to reach the man so he could beat the man into the ground, grind the man into the pavement under his heel like a tar stain.

All this happened in mere moments. And before Travis reached the near edge of the parking lot, the man caught sight of his motion, turned, and saw what was coming at him: an angry lover, US Government–trained in the art of dealing death.

Big as he was, thick as he was, the bullying thug took a reluctant step back from Jennifer where she cowered away from him. Baring his teeth in frustrated rage, he yanked open the door of the SUV behind him. With a last sneer at the onrushing Travis, he quickly got into the vehicle.

That's when Travis finally reached the macadam, so he could really dash. But it was too late. The SUV's red taillights flared. With a screech of smoking rubber, the vehicle swung backward out of its parking space. It shot forward, turned, and was at the lot exit before Travis was halfway across. Travis couldn't read the license plate from there. He couldn't tell the make of the vehicle. All these black SUVs looked alike.

Another screech of tires and the thug was gone.

Then Travis reached Jennifer. She collapsed into his arms, gasping for breath as he held her head against his chest.

Winter was now driving in that daydream state where a man seems divided, body from mind. The snow continued heavy. The windshield wipers flipped back and forth. The sky vanished, and the highway grew black. The snow began to pile up on the shoulders and the guardrail. The physical part of Winter drove with attention and skill through the storm, but the inner man was far away, back in that summer, back in that parking lot, where Travis and the remarkable woman he loved confronted each other in the aftermath of the incident.

"Who was that?" he demanded of her.

"I don't know. I don't know. He attacked me."

"Jennifer, you knew him. Was that the man you told me about? The bad relationship?"

She hesitated. "Yes," she said. But with a surge of nausea, Travis realized she was seizing on the explanation. She was lying to him.

When she looked up and saw the expression on his face—his realization and dismay—she shook her head at him. "Darling, don't. Please."

"He was absolutely crushed," May told Winter. "It was like he couldn't get a break. Here, finally, this beautiful person had come into his life—had come into Lila's life—and Travis adored Lila more than anything—and here she had come into their lives and brought them back from almost, like, the dead, like when a plant dies and you nurse it back and it blooms again. And Travis had been beginning to hope there could still be something good for him in life. And now this happened instead."

"He must have wondered," Winter said to her, choosing his words carefully. "He already had a feeling that she wouldn't talk to him, that she wouldn't even tell him about her childhood—so didn't he wonder what all this meant?"

"Oh my God," said May. "He was obsessed with it."

It wasn't just the lie Jennifer had told, she said, though that was very terrible to him. And it wasn't just the unknowing: the secret that had been standing between them all summer long like a transparent barrier, felt but not seen, and had now suddenly become solid, visible, a brick wall.

It was jealousy. It was jealousy more than anything. Travis felt jealousy writhing in his guts like a lizard beast, devouring him from within.

Because May was right. Jennifer had given him his life back, given his daughter her father back and her childhood back. He wasn't just in love with her, he was clinging to her like driftwood in the stormy sea. And now who was this man who felt free to put his hands on her? To leave a bruise on her? Why wouldn't she tell him so he could help her, protect her? Why was she shielding this terrible man?

"Could it have been a relative?" Winter asked May. "Could the man have been her father maybe?"

May shook her head. "Travis wanted to believe that, but there was no resemblance—he could see that even from a distance and also . . ."

"What?"

May sighed. "He said there was just something about the way the man touched her. The way she let him touch her. The way she cowered when he was leaning over her. It was like he owned her. Like she knew he owned her. Like they both knew."

So this became the center of their autumn together. Travis could not leave it alone, and Jennifer would not satisfy his hunger to know the truth. He could not sleep.

He could not stop questioning her. It made her cry finally.

"Please, Travis. Please stop."

"Is that why you think he killed her?" Winter asked May.

"I know it is," May said. "The jealousy. It drove him insane."

The snow tapered quickly and then stopped as suddenly as it had started and there was Sweet Haven on the road in front of him. Winter, the English professor, smiled ruefully to himself when he saw the scene. The "objective correlative" is a literary technique in which emotions are represented by outward symbols—as a lightning storm in a story might represent a character's inner turmoil, say. Here, as he escaped the gray city that had seemed almost a manifestation of his melancholy, the blizzard ended and the Christmas-card town of Sweet Haven appeared in all its haven-y sweetness. It gleamed under a blue sky complete with a rainbow arching over the lake. Even at this distance, there was something cloying about it. It was not entirely convincing.

Then Winter's phone finally rang and it was—finally—Victoria.

"You better come to my office," she said. "We found the real Jennifer Dean."

12

"It's like some sort of horror-movie version of a fairy tale," Victoria told him. "She was like a princess locked in the evil wizard's tower."

Winter made only a murmured sound as he pored over the documents. Victoria had printed them out and spread them over every space she could find. The public defender's office on the second floor of the county courthouse was not exactly expansive. Two desks close together, a whiteboard on one wall, and an outer alcove for the assistant; that was all there was. Now almost all of it was buried under documents.

The descriptions on the pages were terse. The language was bland federal officialese. There was not much detail, and whole pages were blacked out—*redacted* to use the DC term. But Victoria was right: as Winter read them, what came into his mind was the book he had seen in the school library, the book Jennifer had written and illustrated for the children, the fairy tale about the ghost in the tower.

Jennifer's real name, it turned out, was Anya Petrovna. She had been kidnapped from her school in Kiev at the age of sixteen. She had been brought to the United States and essentially imprisoned in a mansion hidden in the Hollywood Hills above Los Angeles. A security guard informed her she was now the property of Mikhail Oblonsky. Oblonsky was a former KGB agent who had gone gangster after the Soviet Union fell. Ultimately, he had taken over the West Coast branch of the Russian mafia.

There was a photo of Oblonsky on one of the pages. He was a three-hundred-pound monster. His hairy body was covered with tattoos. His face was something like the face of a jungle god carved out of stone. His acts of violence were legendary. His enemies didn't die, they vanished, leaving nothing behind but whispered stories about the intricate torments they had suffered before the light of life went out.

But Oblonsky hadn't brought Anya to America for himself. She was a gift for his son, Grigor. There was a photo of Grigor in the documents too. He was young and muscular, also hairy, also tattooed. He had a head shaped like a wedge, thick at the brow, pointed at the chin. His face was the face you would see if you had a nightmare about a Russian gangster. He was savage, certain, dead-eyed. When Oblonsky's enemies vanished, it was Grigor who arranged the vanishing. He enjoyed his work. The screaming made him laugh.

But Grigor was a worry to his father. He was wild. He was also stupid. He took drugs. He talked too much. He slept around. There were rumors that not everyone he slept with was, strictly speaking, female. There were rumors that some of these not-female bed partners had also vanished after they tried to blackmail Grigor by threatening to tell his father.

His father did not believe these rumors, except deep in his heart where he did believe them. He decided what Grigor needed was to settle down with a good virgin bride from the homeland. So he kidnapped one. Anya.

Oblonsky visited Anya in the small tower bedroom where she was imprisoned. He sat his tremendous bulk down on a chair in front of her. With his huge legs spread and one fist planted on one knee, he calmly explained to her what would happen after she married Grigor. She would have wealth untold. She would have enormous prestige in the Russian community. Then he explained to her, also calmly, what would happen if she refused to marry Grigor or otherwise thwarted his plans. Oblonsky's explanation was very detailed. Anya curled up on her bed as far from him as she could get and wept with terror.

Winter finished one report and pulled another down from the whiteboard on the wall. He sprawled in a desk chair and paged through it. Now and then, he glanced up at Victoria. She sat in her own desk chair, sometimes paging through another report, sometimes just watching him read. They sighed and shook their heads at each other. Poor Anya. Poor Jennifer Dean.

Anya's marriage to Grigor had been three years of boredom punctuated by sudden moments of violence and fear. The only blessing was that there wasn't much sex involved, which was a relief, because her greatest anxiety was that she would be forced to give life to the spawn of this inhuman devil. Mostly he kept her locked away in the hideous concrete fortress that was his Hollywood Hills home. She passed the time watching television. She perfected her English by watching the news. She taught herself the culture by watching movies and TV shows.

It was while watching a cop show that she first learned about WITSEC—the Witness Security Program run by the United States Marshals Service.

Here, a portion of the record was blacked out. Winter glanced up at Victoria again, raising one eyebrow in question.

"If you think it was easy wresting this stuff from the feds, you're wrong," she told him. "First I had to get them to admit that Jennifer was Anya. Then I had to convince them that she was dead. Then, even after they confirmed she was dead, they kept saying they didn't want to expose their super-duper top secret techniques."

Winter stuck his tongue in his cheek and sat thinking. He did not want to undercut Victoria's sense of achievement by telling her she never would have gotten the documents at all without Stan "Stan-Stan" Stankowski working behind the scenes. He kept silent. His mind drifted. His hand—the hand holding the printout—sank over the side of the chair arm. He stared into space.

After a while, Victoria asked him, "What? What are you thinking?"

Coming back to himself, he looked at her. His first thought was that she still resembled a cheerful high school girl, freckles and all. There must have been some well of innocence within her, even now, he thought, to keep her looking so young. The thought distracted him. His eyes went over her tenderly.

She smiled and flushed a little as if she had read his thoughts, which she probably had.

"Come on. What's on your mind?" she said with a laugh.

He shook his head. "The other man. The man Travis Blake was obsessed with. The one he says he killed her over."

"What about him?"

"Did he tell you about their day at the beach?"

"Agh!" Vic dropped her head back, closed her eyes, and opened her mouth with exasperation. After a moment or so of that, she came forward, elbows on the desk, hands supporting her forehead. "No. He hardly tells me anything. God forbid I should actually be able to defend him."

"That's what started it," said Winter. "The man at the beach. He accosted her and Travis saw it."

"What did the man say?"

"Travis was out of earshot and Jennifer—Anya—wouldn't tell him. That's what drove him nuts."

Victoria cursed. She should have known about this, but she hadn't. "Was he one of these types? One of these Russians?"

"That's what I was wondering," Winter said. "I don't think he was one of these particular guys anyway—any of these guys in the pictures. There was apparently something wrong with his face."

"They've got the faces of evil psychopaths, does that count?"

He snorted a laugh. "I don't think so. Anyway, he didn't act like one of these guys. He shook her but he didn't hurt her. He ran when Travis came after him. These guys don't strike me as runners."

Victoria only nodded vaguely in answer. She was obviously still thinking about the fact that her client hadn't told her about the incident at the beach. Winter went back to reading. She watched his face. She could see some emotion or some chain of thought working its way through him. But for now she didn't question him anymore. For now she let him read.

He read: Anya decided to escape. She decided she would gather evidence against Grigor and make her way to the feds and have them put her in the WITSEC program she had heard about on television.

She began to search the house. She read documents. She listened in on phone calls. She found the combination to a safe. She found the safe under a floorboard in the rec room. Inside the safe, she found more documents and a cache of photographs and memory sticks. The photographs were souvenirs of some of the murders Grigor had committed.

All of this took tremendous courage on her part. She was still only nineteen—nineteen, then twenty. Her house was filled with security men day and night. There were cameras around the perimeter. She was not allowed to go anywhere alone. When she went to the gym, when she went shopping, there was always a thug trailing behind her, sometimes two. Her phone calls and internet activity were monitored. Old Man Oblonsky had explained to her that she would not be safe even if she went to the police. "We have many friends on the police," he told her.

She believed him. But she knew her husband was afraid of the feds. She had heard him speaking about them. She told herself if she could get to the FBI with her documents and pictures, they would put her in the WITSEC program and she would finally be free.

Her escape from the mobster's fortress was a masterpiece of strategy and daring. She believed the thugs who guarded her drank on the job. She wasn't absolutely certain, but she believed it. They all had thermoses filled with coffee, and she believed the coffee was laced with vodka. Once again, the report was redacted here, so it was not quite clear how Anya planned to spike one guard's coffee and vodka with her prescription sedatives, but apparently that was the plan.

But it was not the whole plan. She couldn't drug all the guards in the house—the guards and the servants and the guards down by the front gate. Instead, she settled on Viktor. Viktor was the guard who often doubled as her chauffeur. He was wiry and muscular but smaller than some of the other thugs, so she thought he'd be easier to sedate. She began to ask him now and then to drive her up to the top ridge of Runyon Canyon so she could see the sunset over the city. Whenever she did this, he watched her from inside the car. He always drank a lot of coffee while he watched.

She chose a day in January when sundown came early, around five o'clock. She asked to go out about an hour before that, around four. She sat on the brow of the ridge as she always did. Viktor watched her from the car and drank coffee.

The sun arced down toward the horizon. The blue Los Angeles sky gathered itself into a deeper blue. Anya sat hugging her knees and watching the skyline. Her heart was pounding in her chest as if it were demanding to be set free.

It was around 4:30 when Viktor must have realized he'd been drugged. He got out of the car. It took him three tries to get the door open. Then he rose up in the doorway, dazed, unsure where the threat had come from, fumbling in his fear and confusion for the gun under his jacket. He was fighting to stay awake, but Anya had slipped enough sedatives into his drink to knock an elephant senseless. Even as he stepped out of the car, Viktor dropped down on one knee. His fingers scrabbled at the car door for support as he wilted down and down until he was sitting in the dust. His chin fell forward onto his chest. His hand went slack. The gun tumbled out of it.

There were more redactions at this point, whole pages blacked out. But somehow Anya had made her getaway and reached the federal building in Westwood. She had brought the feds enough evidence to give them probable cause to raid Grigor's concrete fortress. She had instructed them where to find the rest of the evidence once they were inside.

Grigor was arrested and charged with two counts of murder. He had killed trial witnesses—that made the murders federal crimes. The feds tacked on some interstate sex trafficking charges as well.

Anya never had to testify in open court. When it became clear that a trial would put his father's enterprises in danger, Grigor pled guilty. Given the fact that Viktor, the chauffeur, had vanished without any trace that was likely ever to be found, this was probably a wise choice on Grigor's part. Oblonsky's paternal feelings only went so far.

Grigor was sentenced to life in prison. Anya was given witness protection: a new name, a new home, a new job, a new life.

Leaning forward in his chair and stretching his arm out, Winter now snagged the final report from the far corner of the gunmetal desk. These were the pages that listed the details of Anya's WITSEC identity. They were almost entirely blacked out. All that was left was the signature of one Brandon Wright, the US Marshal who had overseen Anya's resettlement, and the new name Anya had been given: Angela Wilson.

Winter made a noise. He slumped back in his chair. He pressed his palm against his forehead. "Angela Wilson?" he said.

Victoria had been waiting for this reaction. "I know," she said. "So where did Jennifer Dean come from?"

Winter gave an elaborate sigh. "Not from the feds, I take it."

"They say Angela Wilson went off the grid after seven years. They haven't seen her in three."

"So someone must have made her. Someone made her and she was on the run, like I said."

"Why didn't she just go back to WITSEC for a new identity?"

Winter didn't answer. With his palm still on his forehead, he used his other hand to wave the blacked-out document at her. "Did Travis know about any of this, do you think?"

"He hasn't said so. But really, your guess is as good as mine."

"Can you get his sentencing postponed?"

"Not a chance. The judge wants this done by Christmas. Anyway, what good would it do?"

"I need to talk to him."

"To Travis? I already asked him if you could. He refused. He just wants this over with."

"This story, though," said Winter. "It's too strange. Too deep. There's a motive here I'm missing. Something I'm missing. Something that doesn't make sense. Maybe none of it makes sense."

"Do you think there's any chance Travis is innocent?"

"No," said Winter. "It's not that. He wouldn't risk going to prison for life if he were innocent."

The room was silent then as Winter let his mind work and Victoria sat still, watching him.

Finally, he straightened in his chair. She straightened in her chair, waiting to hear what he would say.

"What about this guy Brandon Wright?" he said. "Do you think he'd talk to us?"

She blinked. "The marshal? No idea. I doubt it. The WITSEC people are incredibly closemouthed. For obvious reasons."

Winter pointed at the computer on her desk. "Search him."

She tapped in the name. "Here's something. Just a story in the local paper about him being selected for the Marshals Service off his police force about a dozen years ago . . ."

Her voice trailed off mid-sentence. When Winter glanced at her, she was staring at the monitor, her features strangely set and serious.

"What's wrong?" he asked her.

It was a moment before she answered. Then, as if she had forgotten he was there and now suddenly remembered, she blinked and turned to him. "What did you say about that man at the beach? The one who threatened Jennifer?"

Winter tried to remember. "Oh. That something was wrong with his face," he said.

Jennifer turned the computer around and showed him the picture of US Marshal Brandon Wright.

13

Another long drive to another gray city. Chicago this time. The sky was blue above snow-covered fields the whole way. And the whole way, she haunted him. Jennifer Dean. The ghost of Jennifer Dean. The image of her face.

What it must have taken for her to become herself, he thought, what resources of both courage and tenderness. A sixteen-year-old girl kidnapped from her home a world away. Nearly four years a prisoner in a nightmare of abuse. A heroic escape. And then—what?—ten years later, she walked into Sweet Haven and she had become extraordinary.

He remembered that video of her reading to the children in the school library, how their faces turned up to her, mesmerized not by the story, he thought, but by her presence. Little Lila had been charmed back to life by her presence. Travis Blake had been made whole by her presence—and then made mad by it, by his jealous need to possess it.

What manner of woman was this? The question kept running through his mind. What manner of woman . . . ?

He drove. He pictured Jennifer Dean in Travis's arms. He pictured himself as Travis. He shook his head to make the pictures disappear.

Maybe it was these therapy sessions with Margaret Whitaker, but something was beginning to shift inside him. He could feel it. Hard as he clung to his melancholy, it was slipping away, slipping like a mask to reveal—what? No, he knew the answer: an almost unbearable yearning. Wasn't that the real subtext of the story he kept telling Margaret, the story about Charlotte and those Christmases so long ago? Wasn't he trying to tell her—to reveal to her—his intolerable loneliness—his excruciating hunger to be loved?

Well, why not? Why not reveal it? Why should he be ashamed of wanting love like any other man?

But he knew, didn't he? He knew exactly why he should be ashamed.

I've killed people, Margaret.

Even that was a dodge. Even that was meant to hide the truth from her. Because most of the people he'd killed deserved killing, and in his own quiet way, Winter was a hard man who did not regret doing what had to be done.

But there was one killing he did regret. One woman. Dead because of him. Because he had drawn her into his bed with a purpose. Because he had convinced her to bring him information. Because her masters had found out and tortured her. And it was only after he had found her body that he was able to admit to himself that he had loved her.

He could not bear to tell Margaret Whitaker that story. So he told her about Charlotte instead. About the ghost, and the graveyard. Which, in the end, was the same story in its way. That's what Charlotte realized that day at the graveyard: her father's ghost story was a story of love, revelation, and betrayal. And that made it the same story as Winter's story in disguise.

He reached Chicago and headed for the North Side. Brandon Wright's apartment was in Rogers Park, near the lake. It was on the third floor of an old brick building on the main drag. There was an Italian trattoria on the ground floor.

It had not been easy to track the man there. Wright had retired from the Marshals Service five years before, and no one seemed to know or care where he'd gone. When Winter and Victoria finally found his contact information, they phoned him for a full day and got no answer. Now Winter stood at the door beside the trattoria and rang the doorbell and got the same results.

He tried the super's bell instead. The super buzzed him in at once. They met in the foyer by the front stairs. The super was a short, round, maybe-Mexican named Sanchez. He had venal eyes and an easy manner, both of which Winter appreciated, thinking they might come in handy.

"He's spending the winter in Florida," Sanchez said. "I think he's thinking about moving there."

"So the place here is empty?"

"His son comes in from time to time, picks up the mail."

"Does he pay the rent too?"

"No, that's transferred right from the bank."

"Did he leave a contact number?"

Sanchez shook his head. "I just call the son if I need anything. I can give you his number if you want. He said I should give out his number if anyone asked about his father. His name is Charlie. Charlie Wright."

Winter took the number. He stood just inside the building's front door and called. While he waited for an answer, he gazed absently through the door's glass pane out at the street. The shops across the way were dense with colorful Christmas lights. Pedestrians passed back and forth. He could only see them from the chest up. Their cheeks were red with cold and their breath came out of their mouths as steam.

"Yuh," came the answer. A thick voice with a grim accent.

"Mr. Wright?" said Winter. "Charlie Wright?"

There was a pause, then: "Yuh. Who's this?"

"My name is Cameron Winter. I'm at your father's apartment building. I need to talk to him about a case he handled when he was with the US Marshals Service. A woman named Anya Petrovna. It's very important."

There was another pause, longer this time. Then Charlie Wright said: "Okay. I'll meet you there. Fifteen minutes."

This time it was Winter who hesitated. But finally he said: "All right. I'm going to give the phone to Mr. Sanchez. Could you ask him to let me into the apartment so I can wait there for you?"

This final pause was so long it was practically eerie. *Who the hell is this guy?* Winter thought.

Then the man said: "All right. I'll tell him. Wait for me in the apartment."

Sanchez took the phone and listened. Then he led Winter upstairs. He unlocked the apartment for him, let him in, and left him there.

The moment the door shut, Winter began to search the place. Fifteen minutes, he thought. That wasn't a lot of time before the man who called himself Charlie Wright showed up and killed him.

The apartment was small but clean enough. Everything in it was cheap and modern: the furniture, the cabinets, the bathrooms, the kitchen counters. Winter went through the closets and the bureau drawers. That took him about four of his fifteen minutes. There wasn't much to see. The closets were full of men's clothes and so were the drawers. There were pictures of Brandon Wright in his Marshals uniform here and there. There was indeed something wrong with the man's face. He'd been badly burned at some point. His features were darkened and smudged as if someone had tried to erase them but hadn't done a thorough job.

Winter studied the pictures one by one. That took another three minutes. Sometimes there were other men in the pictures. But there were no pictures of a wife or children. No pictures of a son. No sign of any Charlie Wright.

With every minute he searched the place, the tension inside him grew. It was like a knot tightening in his stomach. His heart beat faster and faster. The man on the phone had had a Russian accent. Winter now felt certain he was not Brandon Wright's son. He wasn't absolutely sure what the Russian man would do when he arrived, but the possibilities ranged from unpleasant to fatal, with unpleasant-then-fatal being the most likely.

Now he'd been there twelve minutes. That was it: he felt about as wound up as he was willing to feel. He stopped searching the place and stood at the window. He looked down at the urban Christmas scene below. The streetlamps were wrapped in striped paper so they looked like giant candy canes. Life-size toy soldiers stood in the island between one sidewalk and the other. He watched the people passing. Their chins were tucked low against the bitter Chicago wind. Their hands were shoved deep in the pockets of their overcoats.

Then the black car pulled up, a Mercedes. Winter knew it was the Russian even before he stepped out. When he did step out, Winter decided it was time to go, and go quickly. The Russian was about Winter's height but broader. Even covered in a heavy black leather overcoat, he looked substantial. Studying the long, sullen face under the black watch cap, Winter was willing to bet the man had considerable fighting skills. Studying the line of his overcoat, Winter was also willing to bet he was carrying a gun.

Winter headed quickly for the apartment door. As he stepped out into the hall, he heard the front door open downstairs. He went to the end of the hall and stepped through the door there into the fire stairwell. He hurried down the two flights and came out of the building through the side door. Glancing over his shoulder, he walked swiftly through the cold to his SUV.

He drove away, feeling he had escaped a tough Russian thug who had been planning to do him harm.

By the end of the next day, he had discovered this was only partly true. The man was, in fact, a tough Russian thug. And he had, in fact, been planning to do him harm.

But Winter had not escaped.

14

The next day was Saturday. Winter checked out of his hotel in Sweet Haven and drove home to the capital. He dropped in on his apartment to check his mail and get some fresh clothes. Then he headed out and walked over to the university.

The skies were growing gray again as afternoon came on. The quad was deserted to the wind and the fallen snow. In the emptiness, the school's brick castles and stone temples had the aspect of an undiscovered ruin, a dead city of once-noble aspirations lost to the toll of time.

Winter's office was in the building the students called "the Gothic." It was a looming stone edifice of arches and gables and castle towers. It seemed haunted even during the busy semesters when it was full of teachers and students. Today, abandoned to the silence of the coming Christmas, it seemed there could only be ghosts in there. If there weren't ghosts already, Winter thought, he, given his mood, would bring the ghosts in with him.

His footsteps set up a hollow echo in the empty hallways, and on the stairs, too, as he climbed to the second floor. He unlocked his office and went in. It was a tiny box of a place. He had to struggle out of his shearling and force his way behind a chair to hang it on a hook. He had to turn half sideways to edge between the crowded bookshelf and the wooden desk—a desk buried under books and papers. He had to squeeze down into his swivel chair because there was barely room for the chair between the desk and the window.

Despite the cramped quarters, he liked working here, especially during the holidays when the building was all but silent. The internet was spectacularly fast and all his university research resources were available here, whereas some could not be used off campus.

He powered up his computer and downloaded the materials Victoria had sent him: the discovery materials from Travis Blake's prosecutor. He went through the witness statements, the police reports, and Travis's confession.

"I begged her to tell me the truth," Travis had told the police. "I asked her for months and months.

I don't know why I picked up the knife. I guess I meant to threaten her. She still wouldn't tell me. I guess I was half crazy at that point. I couldn't stand it anymore. I stabbed her before I could stop myself."

Finally, there was the video from the security cam at the marina: the man with the rolled-up rug. The video was taken in the dark of a winter night, but the security lights were on and Winter could see clearly that it was Travis with the rug over his shoulder.

Winter watched the video all the way through. Travis had to put the rug down to unlock the gate to the pier where his boat was. As Victoria had said, the rug wasn't quite big enough to hide what was inside it, and when he put it down, it unrolled a little. Winter could see what the police had seen: a glimpse of hair and face. The discovery package included another video with the picture enlarged, and a series of still photos of the body in the rug. There were also some photos of Jennifer Dean for comparison.

Winter went through all the material and nodded to himself. Whether she was Anya Petrovna or Angela Wilson or Jennifer Dean, that was her—her body—rolled up in the rug.

When he finished going through the materials, he closed the files. He sat back in his chair. The space was so tight, he had to use force to swivel around to face the window. Then he sat with his hands folded on his belly and looked out across the quad. He could see the stone tower of the carillon rising above the columned temple of the administration building. The gray clouds moved and thickened behind them, darkening the snow-covered grass. Winter gazed at the scene until he stopped thinking altogether.

This was that strange habit of mind he sometimes talked about: his ability to let go of all his opinions and simply be with the facts of the matter for a while. It was not pure reason that solved puzzles for him, but an odd drifting atmosphere of mingled logic and imagination that seemed to pass across his brain like a mist. He sat there gazing out the window and living in that mist without a single thought he could have put into words. Then, after a while, he blinked as if awakening. The mist passed, and he found he knew almost everything he needed to know.

Again, he maneuvered the chair so he could swivel back to the desk. He powered down the computer. He stood and squeezed his way between the bookshelves and the messy desk. He worked back into his shearling coat. He returned to the office door and pulled it open.

The Russian was there. He pointed a .22 at Winter's forehead, sneered, and pulled the trigger.

15

It was an assassin's weapon: a Scorpion pistol with a modular suppressor. The Russian had the suppressor at full length, so that it was nearly touching Winter's forehead. There was no chance he would miss his target.

If the Russian hadn't sneered, Winter would have been dead on the spot. But the sneer took half a second, and half a second was all Winter needed: that's how fast he was. Even taken completely by surprise, he was able to slam the door into the gunman's arm, hard. It hit his wrist. The pistol went flying from his hand even as it fired almost silently, a muted snap. The bullet passed inches to the right of Winter's face.

The Russian was fast too. He knew at once the gun was beyond recovery. It had tumbled off somewhere into the cramped office. He didn't pause to regret it but simply charged through the door. His big body smacked into Winter full force, carrying him back into the little room.

Winter grunted as his spine hit the desk. The Russian was on top of him. Winter only just managed to catch the Russian's wrist before the thug could close his fingers on his neck and tear his throat open. Winter, meanwhile, tried to slug the thug in the floating rib, but the thug was wearing that black leather overcoat and it softened the blow. The Russian brought his other hand up, trying to get at Winter's eye, but Winter caught the strike on his forearm and blocked it.

Winter heaved off the desk, hurling the Russian into the bookshelves. The Russian wouldn't let go and carried Winter with him. Volumes tumbled down around the two men. The room was silent except for the sound of the books falling and the two men grunting with effort. They were both big, both strong, both well-trained fighters. But now they were wedged in the impossible space between the bookshelf and the edge of the desk, and neither could get off a powerful blow. They grappled there, stuck in place. More books fell off the shelf and dropped down around them. Papers spilled off the desk. Some papers flew up and wafted through the air.

The Russian worked his hand under Winter's chin and tried to force it through to his throat. Winter's hand found a heavy volume on the shelf—a hardcover of the complete poems of Lord Byron. He seized the book and slammed the binding into the side of the Russian's head, once, twice, again. But in that narrow space, he couldn't put any force into the blows. The Russian's head jerked to the side each time he was hit, but he kept on trying to shove his hand under Winter's chin to choke him. Finally, Winter thought to bring the book down into the crook of the Russian's elbow. That broke the thug's grip, and Winter followed through by bringing the edge of Lord Byron up into the Russian's nose.

The thug's nostrils spit blood, and he stumbled backward. Papers flew everywhere. More books came flapping off the shelf.

Winter threw the Byron at the Russian. The Russian tried to duck and lost his balance. He went over sideways, striking his head on the back of the swivel chair. The swivel chair swiveled, and the Russian fell past it, down to the floor. Winter dropped on top of him. The Russian couldn't maneuver in that narrow corner, and Winter rose up and punched him five times in the face with those two knuckles that had been hardened and enlarged by years of fist push-ups on concrete. The sound of his knuckles striking flesh and bone were loud in the surrounding silence. He saw the Russian's eyes cloud over and his jaw go slack.

Then, as quickly as he could, Winter grabbed hold of the desk and pulled himself upright, trying to get his feet under him. A couple of books under his hand slipped off the edge of the desk, and Winter nearly fell. But he managed to work his way back into the narrow space between the desk and the bookshelf.

By now, the Russian was recovering, reaching up to grab both the desk and the windowsill so he could pull himself off the floor. His eyes and teeth were white through the mask of blood that covered his face.

Winter stumbled around the desk. The papers and books under his feet made the path slippery and treacherous. The Russian was almost standing now, almost ready to come after him again.

Winter looked around desperately for the gun.

The Russian roared as he got to his feet. He knocked the computer out of the way and hurled himself over the desk at Winter, his white eyes wide in his gore-darkened face.

But he was too late. Winter had spotted the gun in the corner, directly under the coat hook. He rushed for it. The Russian reached out and grabbed his arm as he passed, but Winter yanked free and went down on his knee and retrieved the Scorpion.

The Russian scrambled over the desk and spilled to the floor on the other side. He shot up quickly to his knees, but there was Winter standing over him, the silenced pistol leveled at his head. The Russian froze in place.

"What's your name?" said Winter breathlessly.

The thug didn't answer. He just knelt there, panting.

"You think I won't kill you?" Winter said.

"You won't," said the Russian.

Winter laughed.

The Russian reconsidered. "I am Popov," he said.

"You work for Oblonsky?"

"I did."

"And now?"

"I am in Chicago now."

"Where's Brandon Wright?"

"I don't know."

"You're lying. Where is he?"

"I do not know."

Winter made a threatening gesture with the gun, but he realized the thug was right: he was not going to kill him. Not in cold blood like this. Not that it wasn't in him to do it. It was. He'd done worse. But this was not then.

Popov seemed to read his mind. Despite the blood smeared all over his face, he smiled. He began to labor to his feet.

Winter didn't bother to tell him to stop. What was the point of making threats when they both knew he wasn't going to shoot unless he had to? He supposed he could threaten to call the police. He supposed he could actually call them. But no, he wasn't going to do that either. Not now, when he was just beginning to get at the truth. The police were the last people he wanted involved.

Instead, he simply drew the gun back close to his side, out of the thug's reach.

Popov stood. He wiped the blood off his mouth with his hand then wiped his hand on his black leather jacket. The two men looked at each other. They were both still breathing hard.

"What did you come here for, then?" Winter asked him.

Popov made a dismissive sound, blowing air and blood out of one side of his mouth. He turned away and shuffled painfully to the door.

"At least tell me why you tried to kill me," Winter said.

Popov opened the door. But he paused. He looked back at Winter.

"You work for the man who killed Anya, yes?" he said.

"I work for his lawyer," said Winter.

"Well, stop," said Popov.

He walked out of the office, shutting the door behind him.

PART THREE

AN ELEMENTAL THING

That Christmas—the Christmas we discovered Charlotte's mother buried in that churchyard in Geneva—that was the last Christmas I ever spent with her, the last I ever spent at Mia's house. In some ways, it was my last Christmas altogether. After that, Charlotte went away, and as far as I was concerned, she took the season with her.

But that last one—that last holiday we had together—that was a strange, dreamy, sad affair. I was still processing the outcome of our kiss outside the little house where her family had first lived when they came over from Germany. I was still thinking about the look on Charlotte's face afterward, that look that said: Not now, but maybe someday. *Of course, I had dreamed of more. I had dreamed she would swoon in my arms and cry, "At last, my prince has come," or something of the sort. But deep down, what I'd really expected was outrage and rejection. So in truth, that look of hers was everything I hadn't even dared to hope for.*

All the same, even as I mooned around the Christmas tree, playing the moment over and over in my mind, it began to seep into my teen-boy consciousness that something was terribly wrong in the house that year. Charlotte and her father, Albert, were at odds somehow. They didn't argue or anything like that—not that I witnessed—they just sort of prowled around each other like wary cats. Which was bizarre really, because Charlotte had always adored her father, even in her teens. She loved to fuss over him and tease him in her solemn way and bring him his coffee in the morning and his beer at night. But there was none of that this year. And once or twice, when I found her in the kitchen or saw her alone in her bedroom through the open door, she looked like she'd been crying. Which, again, was not normal with her.

When I come to think of it, that was the first time I ever noticed that strange habit of mind I told you about, that thing that happens to me sometimes when I'm confronted with a mystery. I remember getting ready for bed on Christmas Eve. Sitting on the edge of my bed, undressing, pulling my socks off. And all at once, I found myself doing nothing, just sitting there, just staring into space, one sock on my foot and one in my hand. I wasn't thinking anything, but it was all there in my head, like figures on a landscape with me at the center: Albert's ghost story about the murdered girl, Adelina Weber; the book Charlotte was reading about East Germany; the graveyard behind the little house in Geneva; the grave of Charlotte's mother. It's not that I suddenly understood everything. It never works like that. It's just that I was aware of a new level of clarity, a strong feeling that it all fit together and could be made sense of if I only tried. But instead, I went back to thinking about the look on Charlotte's face after I kissed her. That look that said: Not now, but maybe someday.

Then Christmas was over, and I went back to the city, back to my tutors and the two wealthy socialites who were vaguely aware they were my parents. Charlotte never came to visit anymore after that. I never saw her. In some ways, I think I didn't want to see her. For one thing, my parents' marriage was unraveling and home was not a happy place. But just in general, I didn't want anything to happen between Charlotte and me that would spoil the promise of that kiss.

In the fall, she went away to college. A little liberal arts college in Indiana. Not far, like I said, just a few hours' drive. But when I emailed her there—a friendly email just to say hello—I got no answer. And when Christmas came that year, she did not return home and I was not invited to Mia's house to visit.

I won't tell you this broke my heart, but I didn't forget it either. I went on, you know, as you go on when you're young. I had a passionate romance my seventeenth year, and that occupied my whole mind and the relevant parts of my body for a while. But the fact that she, that Charlotte, was just gone like that, gone not only from my life but from the life of her beloved family, with no contact and no explanation—it changed me. It was sort of a silent trauma, one of those damaging blows that you don't even feel at first, that you only come to understand as a trauma later because of the way it affects you. My heart, after that, was a haunted house, with the ghost of Charlotte in it, the ghost of that kiss, the ghost of that expression on her face when the kiss was over. Ever after, I was not whole somehow. I knew somehow—knew without really knowing—that I would not be whole until I saw her again.

It wasn't until my first year at university that I knew I had to find her. My passionate seventeen-year-old romance had ended by then, and there had been nothing since but a series of brief encounters, enjoyable at the time but more or less depressing when I thought about them afterward. I had begun to sense that something was not right inside me, that I would not be right inside until I saw Charlotte, until I looked her in the eye and saw for myself whether the promise of our kiss would ever be fulfilled or no.

I emailed her in December and told her I was coming to visit. I chose December, obviously, in the hope I could rekindle the Christmasy feelings of old times. To my surprise, I received an answer—the first I'd heard from her since that last visit. It was just a brief note. Charlotte sent me her address and invited me to dinner.

It was to be our last meeting, and it was a nightmare. That's barely even a figure of speech. It was so much like a nightmare I sometimes wonder if it actually happened at all. For one thing, I had caught a cold a few days before our dinner date, and when the day arrived, I had a slight fever. I took some cold medicine in the hope it would clear my head, but instead it made things worse. By evening, the world seemed alien, distant, and weird to me. When people spoke, the sound was muted, like voices in another room. Their faces seemed to drift before me, dreamlike. I felt vague, dazed.

Charlotte was no longer living on campus but had moved to the town nearby. She was in a house in the middle of a row of houses just like it. Neat clapboards each with a front porch and a peaked roof and a strip of grass out in front, all fine places once, now a little past their prime.

I remember it was dark when I parked outside, dark and bitter cold. There was snow on the lawns and a flurry of snow in the air. My heart was thudding as I climbed the porch steps. I knocked on the door and stood waiting, clutching a bottle of wine in my hand, the gift I had brought for dinner. I remember squinching my eyes shut, trying to clear my head and get some clarity through the fever and the cold medicine.

Then I opened my eyes and she was standing in the doorway before me. My Charlotte of old, but not the same. She had dyed her blond hair black for one thing, and it was not braided like it used to be but fell around her exquisite face in a mess of tangles so she looked like a wild gypsy instead of the way she used to look, like a porcelain figurine. And she wasn't dressed as she used to dress either—not as the prim little Dresden housewife she had always seemed. No, she was aggressively modern, braless in a black T-shirt and faded jeans that were shredded at one knee.

She seemed hectic to me from the first moment, but I was so foggy and feverish, I wasn't sure if it was really her or just my strange impression, just the way I was seeing things. She clutched me quickly by one shoulder, darted forward, and pecked me on the cheek. She gave an odd, high little giggle and said, "Look at you, all grown up now, such a big boy."

She stayed on that theme as she led me into the main room. How I was grown up and how she remembered me when I was little and how I was afraid of the dark and she sat on my bed to comfort me—all in a high, rapid-fire patter. It was belittling, infantilizing, like when I was a boy of twelve and she was a young woman all of fourteen, too grand and adult for me to dream of. It certainly had the effect of neutralizing any hopes I had of repeating our kiss. Maybe that was the point of it, I don't know.

She went on in the same vein as she poured me a glass of wine—and on as we sat close together on an old, saggy couch in the living room—and still on as we drank, me gazing into her eyes, trying to find the girl I loved in there.

Each sip of the wine made the world vaguer and stranger and more dreamlike. Images of my surroundings came to me in an impressionistic swirl. A dining table with candles and three places set. The cheap, worn furnishings. No Christmas decorations. None. Just posters on the wall, art prints from museum exhibitions, all of them dark and nightmarish, violent but vibrantly realistic. A lion ripping into the back of a wild-eyed horse. Death sitting on the bed of a maiden, like a mockery of the Annunciation. A knight in a valley crowded with monsters. The images seemed to assault my senses like a madman screaming his delusions into my face. And while Charlotte kept up her frantic chattering—"I remember how your face lit up when you unwrapped that adorable little baseball game!"—I thought to myself: Why are there three places set at the table? Why three?

I soon learned the answer. I don't know exactly how much time passed while we sat there, but not much, maybe fifteen minutes. I had drunk, say, half a glass of wine, just enough, mingled with the cold medicine, to make the whole scene—the room, the posters, this strange new Charlotte with her gypsy hair and her high, giggling, frenetic talk—to make all of it seem phantasmagorical.

Then I heard the front door open.

Charlotte leapt to her feet and cried, "Here's Eddie!"

The way she said it—or the way I heard it—it sounded like the wild, triumphant shriek of some mountain witch who'd just conjured a demon out of the earth.

"Here's Eddie!"

And to add to that impression, there was a sound of skittering claws, and as I swayed to my feet to greet whoever the hell Eddie was, two Dobermans the size of automobiles came slipping and charging into the room.

The moment they spotted me, they set up an insane, throaty clamor of howling and barking. They launched themselves at me as I staggered back in woozy terror. I was driven against the wall. They pinned me there, drooling, snarling, their teeth bared, their raging eyes fastened hungrily on my face.

Then in came Eddie.

He was a small man, five-foot-five or -six. In his thirties. Oddly shaped. He had thin legs under double-wide hips that gave him a rolling, crippled gait. He had over-broad shoulders and huge, powerful arms, almost beastlike. He looked odd enough to me that, normally, I might have felt some sympathy for him, some fellow feeling. And maybe it was only the fever or jealousy that turned my heart cold toward him right off. But I don't think so. It was something about him. The malevolence in the eyes under his thinning, flyaway blond hair, the too-bright smile. In my drugged state, he reminded me of an illustration from some book of German fairy tales I'd had as a child: an evil troll leering from the forest depths.

He was grinning at me where I stood pinned by the dogs. The dogs seemed to me like his familiars.

Charlotte skipped to greet him. He slid one arm around her bottom as if it were her waist, and she leaned into the cloud of his hair, nuzzling him fondly.

They both seemed wholly indifferent to my predicament. The snarling devil dogs. My heart-pounding terror. Charlotte seemed to take no notice at all.

She said fondly, "Cameron, this is Eddie, my boyfriend."

At which point Eddie finally seemed to notice what was happening. He casually shouted in a deep, guttural voice, "Donner! Loki! Halt!"

The dogs glanced at him doubtfully as if hoping they might have misheard him, hoping he had really ordered them to tear me to pieces.

But he repeated it: "Halt! Down!"

They reluctantly broke off their deafening barks and snarls and settled sullenly onto the floor, keeping their fiery eyes trained on me just in case.

"So nice to meet you," Eddie said with what seemed to me demonic malice. "Charlotte has told me so much about her little charge."

Her little charge. Now he was on that theme as well.

All this was only the prelude to the nightmare, though. This was the nightmare before the nightmare began. Soon, we were all three sitting at dinner, with Eddie-My-Boyfriend at the head of the table and Charlotte looking at him worshipfully from the foot and me between them while the dogs from hell prowled dangerously around our legs either hoping for scraps or waiting for the command to rip my crotch out and eat their way up to my throat.

You have to imagine all this taking place in a febrile, dreamlike fog, which only thickened as I kept drinking wine through the cheap pasta dinner. Charlotte continued skirling and giggling away about my child-self, evoking Christmas memories that seemed themselves a dream within the dream. And Eddie—Eddie-My-Boyfriend—would occasionally chime in with some theoretically piercing pseudo-wisdom like the chorus in a stilted theatrical production put on in some fascist state.

Charlotte said something to me like, "Oh, how you loved that little Christmas village with the train going choo-choo-choo, round and round!"

I tried to smile as if I weren't being repeatedly humiliated.

Then, in his guttural mutter, Eddie-My-Boyfriend said, "What a fraud it all turned out to be, eh?"

And I said foggily, "A fraud? Christmas?"

He waved his wineglass around imperiously like he was king of the mead hall. He said, "Christmas in this age of unbelief. The happy family in all this decadence. The whole charade."

And Charlotte, as if her beau had had a flash of insight amounting to genius, said: "Wasn't it? Such a fraud!" Then, seeing the confused look on my face: "Oh, I forgot; you never heard the whole story."

"There is always a whole story," declared Eddie. "You can count on that, believe me. The truth beneath the happy family fantasy."

"The truth beneath the fantasy, exactly," Charlotte said.

"What was the truth beneath the fantasy?" I asked. I was trying to sound grown-up, you know, to counter Charlotte's babying condescension, but I suspect I sounded more like the detective in a mystery movie in that moment when he realizes his drink has been drugged just before he collapses into unconsciousness. I really was confused and couldn't grasp what they were telling me.

"Well, you remember the grave?" said Charlotte in her weirdly high-pitched voice, a voice with an edge of hysteria. "My mother's grave like the grave from the ghost story."

"Adelina Weber," I managed to mutter. "Sure."

"Adelina Weber," Eddie repeated, wagging his finger at me, as if I had said something surprisingly wise for one still so young. "There is always an Adelina Weber buried beneath this dying civilization you're so proud of. Believe

me. And not just one either. There are ranks of buried Adelinas."

I tried to object that I wasn't all that proud of our dying civilization, but I couldn't string the words together.

Instead, I spoke thickly to Charlotte. "She was real, you mean?"

Even in my groggy state, I realized as soon as I had spoken that I knew this already, that I had known at some level that Adelina Weber was real ever since that moment I had sat on the bed holding my sock in my hand and gazing at nothing. It was then I had figured out—or worked out in my unconscious—that the ghost from Albert's story had been a real woman once, and that somehow Charlotte's father was responsible for her death back in East Germany.

"Oh yes," said Charlotte, confirming my thoughts. "She was very real. Even her ghost was real. She haunted my father. My mother too."

"In a way, you see," Eddie-My-Boyfriend pontificated, "in a way, the ghost story was all about Albert, all of it. The policeman who was haunted by the ghost was himself, and so was the father who hunted the poor girl down to her love nest, and so was the lover too. The ghost story was a psychomachia. Every character was himself."

For a moment, I stared at him, at his bright-eyed malice and his wild-haired pomposity. I would have loved, just then, to clutch him by the throat and lift him bodily out of his seat.

I think the dogs read my mind somehow. They growled a dark warning from under the table. To avoid being gutted, I gave up my plan of throttling the man and turned back to Charlotte.

"It's true!" she said. "Daddy was an informer for the Stasi!" She giggled at that—don't ask me why

"They all were," said Eddie, waving it away with a frown. "You have to make accommodations. What else can you do?"

"It's true, they all were," Charlotte sang out gaily. "Or a lot of them, at least, in those days. And my father was with the Vopos, so really, I should have known."

"It's just part of the process," said Eddie. "Once the decay sets in, night follows day."

Now I was gaping at Charlotte. Because I could not understand anything anymore. It was all such a nightmare to me.

"Except my mother," Charlotte said. "She wasn't part of it."

Eddie snorted as if this were somehow absurd.

"No, she wasn't!" Charlotte meekly insisted to him. "She wasn't, Eddie."

Eddie shrugged grimly. "If you say so."

"That's why she was so shocked when Adelina's daughter mailed her copies of the files—the Stasi files, after they were

opened to the public. It was all right there on the page. My father had been Adelina's lover. And he had turned her in to the Stasi for anti-revolutionary activity. She was put in the Bautzner Strasse prison and interrogated—"

"Tortured," said Eddie.

"Tortured, yes. She didn't live very long after that."

"Night follows day," said Eddie-My-boyfriend. "Fear, weakness, decay. Then this is what you become."

"But that wasn't even the joke," Charlotte went on, and she giggled yet again, as if there really was a joke in all this. "The joke was that when my mother confronted my father about what he'd done, you know what his excuse was?"

She waited, looking at me, as if I would try to guess the answer. And Eddie, in the pause, muttered, "There is always something like this, believe me." I could barely understand anything they were saying.

"His excuse," said Charlotte, "was that we wouldn't have gotten out of the country otherwise. Because somehow, Adelina had had jewels, a small cache of jewels, hidden away. She was holding it for an underground group that gathered at her church. It was to fund an escape to the West, I think. My father learned about it during their affair. So by betraying her to the Stasi, you see, he was able to make off with some of the jewels himself. That's how he got the money he needed to get out when he saw the end was coming. When the Soviets abandoned the GDR, and

the Germans started to deport dissidents in order to keep the peace, he was able to bribe our way onto one of the trains and bring us, finally, to America. It was because he betrayed Adelina Weber that we were able to make our escape. I think that was what killed my mother. The fact that she had benefited. That made her part of it too, that made her complicit, even in ignorance. She couldn't stand that. That's what I believe anyway."

"They were all complicit," said Eddie-My-Boyfriend. "It's a process. Believe me."

"Killed . . ." I said heavily. "Killed your mother . . ."

"Well, they called it an accident," Charlotte said—her voice sounded almost gay to me. "Alcohol. Drugs. An overdose. They said it must have been a mistake . . ."

"And they never told you," I said, slurring my words. "They told you she died back in Germany."

Again, Charlotte giggled, as if the irony of it were oh-so-amusing. "I suppose she did, in a way. I suppose she did die back in Germany. She was just the last one to get the news."

Eddie also gave a laugh, a heavy laugh. "Ha. That's very good," he said. And Charlotte beamed, pleased by his approval. And the dogs beneath the table barked once: his familiars. Then Eddie said to me: "Ha. If you could see your face, little Cameron." He laughed again. "It is always like this when the mask comes off. Oh, the shock! The horror! The whole Christmas-happy-family-choo-choo-train-village *is peeled away like wallpaper and what is there beneath? Adelina. The skeleton truth. Night follows day. Your face is really a picture. Believe me."*

But he was wrong, you know. Eddie-My-boyfriend got it wrong altogether, evil little troll that he was. That wasn't what the look on my face was expressing, not at all. I wasn't feeling shock and horror at the hypocrisy and phoniness and decadence of modern life. In fact, in that moment, it didn't seem hypocritical or phony or decadent to me at all. In my drugged haze, my drugged and now drunken haze, in the vortex of dreamlike confusion in which Charlotte and her giggles and her troll lover and his devil dogs all swirled in the fog around me, the only thing that did seem real to me were those Christmases of our childhood, the decorations, the lighted tree, the smell of pastry baking in that pleasant little house, the toy train going choo-choo around the plastic village, and how happy it all made me—and Charlotte and how much I loved her then. It was this—this now—this awful story of betrayal from a past and from a country I had never known—this giddy gypsy Charlotte—this worthless, stunted little man of hers—these beasts sniffing at us on the floor—and the posters, the violent, oppressive posters on the wall—it was all this that seemed unreal and nightmarish, a thin façade of rage and ugliness painted over the one solid reality I could cling to, which was, again, our Christmases, our past together, my love.

I remember stumbling out of there as soon as dinner ended, as soon as I politely could. I remember the dogs howling after me as I left, and Eddie shouting at them, "Halt! Down!" I remember glancing back as I reached my car and seeing the two of them standing in the doorway, the strange little man still holding a glass of wine in one hand, and his other great muscular arm around Charlotte's bottom as if it were her waist.

And Charlotte—black-haired gypsy Charlotte—was smiling her hectic smile as she watched me go, her eyes bright and damp and secretly miserable. I stood just one last moment and searched her face, searched it longingly for some hidden remnant of that expression I remembered, that expression after I kissed her: Not now, but maybe someday.

But I could find no trace of it. There was no someday there. There was no someday at all.

I never saw her again.

16

When Winter finished speaking, Margaret Whitaker sat for a long moment in watchful silence. She was relieved this strange story of his was finally over. Now it was up to her to make something of it, or to help him make something of it. But what?

He was sitting in the client's chair, slumped and slack in his jeans and his white cable-knit sweater. It was as if the effort of speaking had exhausted him. His head was lowered so Margaret couldn't see—she wasn't distracted by—the nearly black bruise on his throat. It worried her. She knew a mark of violence when she saw one. But since he hadn't mentioned it to her, she was biding her time before she asked about it.

He looked up at her from under heavy eyelids. She could read the challenge in his eyes. She knew she would have to proceed with care. This was an intelligent man, an educated, sensitive, insightful man. He had insisted on telling her this weird tale over three full sessions. There had to be a reason for that. It had to be some code, some parable—the only way he could bear to outline for her the dark foundation of his melancholy.

The therapist propped her elbow on her chair arm, propped her chin on her thumb, her index finger up along her temple. "That word," she said. "That word Eddie used. What was it? Psychomachia. I don't think I've ever heard that word before. What does it mean? Do you know?"

Winter drew a deep breath and straightened in his chair. "It means a battle of the mind or of the soul. It's sometimes used in literary studies to discuss a story or a poem in which each character represents a different aspect of a single person. You see it, for instance, in the epic poetry of William Blake. Each of his mythic figures represents part of a single psyche: the creative instinct, the judgmental conscience, the thwarted desire, and so on. You can read him that way anyway."

"I see," said Margaret. "Dreams are like that sometimes. Dreams and fantasies. All the characters represent aspects of the dreamer."

"Right."

"So in a way, it was just as Eddie said, wasn't it? Eddie-My-Boyfriend, as you call him. In Albert's ghost story, Albert was the policeman haunted by Adelina and he was also Adelina's lover, obviously, and also the father—the Stasi—who found her out and killed her. He was even the ghost in some way, I suppose. The ghost was his conscience."

Winter only nodded, gazing blankly into the middle distance.

"What about your story, Cam?" Margaret asked him. "Your story about Charlotte and Mia and Albert and Eddie-My-Boyfriend and the devil dogs. Is that a psychomachia too?"

He smiled vaguely. "It can't be a psychomachia if it really happened, can it? Or I don't know. Maybe it can. The poet Keats said, 'A man's life of any worth is a continual allegory.' So maybe it can."

"Maybe a man's life becomes an allegory when he tells it. It does work like that, you know. We reveal ourselves in the stories we tell."

Winter only grunted softly in response.

Margaret went on studying him. "What is that bruise on your throat?" she asked finally. "Where did you get that?"

He drew a deep breath and let it all out before answering her. "A Russian gangster named Popov tried to kill me."

"Popov . . ." she repeated with a laugh—but then she stopped laughing because she saw it wasn't a joke. "Is this part of that other work you mentioned? Where you track down people who have committed crimes using your—habit of mind?"

"Something like that, yes."

"And this Russian gangster, Popov, didn't want you to track him down?"

Winter cocked his head, thinking. "He didn't want me to track down something anyway."

"You don't know what? You don't know why he tried to strangle you?"

"Actually, I do have a few thoughts. It's all beginning to make sense to me. There's only one thing really I haven't been able to figure out yet."

She didn't answer. She still continued watching him, chin on her thumb, cheek on her finger.

"I think," she said slowly—and now she straightened, and lowered her hand, and clasped it with the other hand in front of her. "I think in this allegorical life of yours, this story about Charlotte and her family, the character of you represents you watching your own mind at work. And Albert is Albert but he's also you—you committing an act of betrayal, some terrible act in your past that perhaps, like Albert's act, got a woman killed for your own gain."

Winter blinked as if she had splashed a glass of ice water in his face. He sat up out of his slouch and stared at her.

"And I think Charlotte is Charlotte," she went on, "but Charlotte is also you, that innocent part of you that sees what you did and fears that it has left you unlovable, unworthy of the love you want so badly. And I think Eddie is Eddie but Eddie and his dogs are you as well. Eddie represents your mind's efforts to intellectualize and distance itself from the terrible act you committed, the death you caused, and the dogs are that part of you that is threatening to devour you with guilt. So now the innocent you and the evil rationalizer you are wedded together—like Eddie and Charlotte."

For another second or two after she was finished, Winter just went on as he was, sitting up straight, staring at her with that startled look on his face. Then he blew out a single puff of air: *Whew!*

"What are you thinking?" she asked him.

Another second of gaping silence went by and then another.

Then Winter murmured: "That's the answer, isn't it?"

"I'm sorry, what?"

"The one thing I couldn't figure out. That's it. You just gave it to me."

Margaret shook her head. She still didn't understand him.

As if it would make all things clear to her, he gestured at her with an open hand.

He said, "I understand now why Travis Blake thought he could get away with murder."

17

Winter left the therapy session and drove directly to Sweet Haven. He traveled quickly. He knew there wasn't much time. As the buildings of the capital fell away behind him, the sky ahead filled the Jeep's big windshield: an angry sky, dark with the coming of snow.

Winter drove toward the storm. His feelings were in a jumble. This woman, this therapist, Margaret Whitaker—she troubled him. The way she saw into him, the way she exposed him. He wanted to tell himself that he didn't like it, that he ought to cancel the sessions. But that simply wasn't true. He did like it. It was painful, but he could feel it working in him for the good. His melancholy was lifting. His guilt, his shame, and the longing that lay underneath the sadness were coming into the open, beginning to soften in the light. If Margaret Whitaker could see into him so completely—if she could see all that he was and yet not cast him out of her office into the exterior darkness—then perhaps he was not as unlovable as he had come to fear.

And now, also, her insights had given him the last piece of the puzzle: the full truth about Travis Blake.

It was quarter to three when he reached the little city. He only had fifteen minutes to spare. He drove swiftly down the main lane, past the Christmas-card scene of quaint storefronts draped with evergreen boughs and lights and pictures of Santa. He parked his SUV half a block away from the stately county offices and the courthouse. He hurried the rest of the distance on foot, weaving through shoppers in their winter coats.

As he speed-walked through the courthouse halls, he noticed again what Victoria had described to him: the military presence nearly everywhere. The policemen in the halls were former soldiers. So were the prosecutors, and even some of the clerical staff. They all had the straight-yet-easy carriage of fighting men. It was like being back on one of the Forward Operating Bases he had sometimes stayed in overseas.

He was out of breath when he pushed into the courtroom on the second floor, but he'd made it: there was still half an hour before the sentencing hearing was scheduled to begin. He could see the hearing was going to be crowded. There were already people filling the pews. Many of these were soldiers, mostly in service uniforms but some in full dress with their medals on their chests. Nichola Atwater, the school principal, was there as well. She had gotten a place up front. She was seated next to another woman, a younger blonde. Winter guessed that was Hester, the mother of little Lila's friend Gwen.

Mrs. Atwater turned in her seat when he came in. She nodded to him solemnly. He nodded back. Then he spotted Victoria. She was waiting for him by the side door across from the jury box, the door that led to the holding cells.

As he hurried to her, he saw how weary she looked, her normally bright eyes dull, the freckles standing out on her wan cheeks. It gave him a pang to see all that high school cheer drained out of her by this impossible case—a case that troubled her instincts but defied her reason.

Her glance went to his neck. He'd told her about Popov's attack, but this was the first time she'd seen the bruises. "Oh God, Cam," she said.

"It's all right. It's fine."

"And you still don't know what he was after?"

He didn't answer. He didn't want to lie. He just said: "Is Travis still willing to see me?"

She sighed. "He's not happy about it, but he hasn't said no. Listen, if you can, talk him out of making a statement, an allocution. He won't listen to me. It'll only make things worse."

"I doubt I'll have much influence with him."

Victoria sighed again in answer. She rapped softly on the thick wooden door. A bailiff opened it from within. The bailiff was another one: crewcut, mustached, an old soldier. He led the way down the hall to the elevator, and down they all went in the elevator, to the cells.

There were three cells. They lined one wall of a dimly lit corridor in the basement. Travis Blake was in the middle one. The others were empty. Blake was standing in the center of the little space—standing perfectly still—standing at attention, Winter thought—staring at the pale green cinder-block wall three feet away from him. He was a big man, bigger than Winter was, more powerful, more muscular. Winter could see this even through his loose-fitting "county orange" jumpsuit. And he still had all his military inner discipline too. He was relaxed. Focused. Waiting.

When the bailiff unlocked the cage, Blake turned his head—he turned only his head; his body remained facing the wall. He looked first at Victoria, his lawyer, then at Winter. The two men locked eyes.

Blake's beard was gone, and his black hair was cut short, but his eyes were just as they'd been described to Winter: pale, icy, cruel. Winter could not imagine how Jennifer Dean had looked in those eyes and seen a father and a lover. But she somehow had.

The icy eyes went up and down Winter's full length, pausing only a moment at the bruise on his throat. Blake grinned.

"They didn't tell me you were a spook," he said.

"I'm an English professor," said Winter.

Travis shrugged. "Whatever."

Winter gave a half smile. He turned to Victoria. He didn't have to speak. They'd arranged it all. She left the cell without a word. Blake watched her go until the bailiff brought the cell door shut with a clang.

Then the two men were alone. Their gazes locked again, neither gaze friendly, neither hostile, just watching.

Travis Blake was the first to look away. His mouth twitched into a sneer for just a second, then straightened.

"All right, then," he said. He brought the cruel eyes back around to Winter. "How much do you know?"

Winter didn't say a word. He let Blake read the answer in his expression. Blake read it.

"What are you going to do?" he asked.

"I haven't decided. You've committed murder under the law, Blake. You know that."

"So you're going to try to stop me."

"I haven't decided," Winter said again.

One corner of Blake's mouth turned up. He seemed amused. "You really think it'll be up to you when the crunch comes?"

Winter considered. "Yes. I do."

"I guess neither one of us is a stranger to killing. But as you say, I've done murder now. That's different. You think I'd hesitate if you got in my way?"

"No, of course not."

"What then? You think you can take me, man to man?"

Winter gave a quick puff of a laugh. "We're not twelve years old, Travis. I'm not going to trade double dares with you."

"You just think I won't do it, is that it? You just think I'll decide not to. I'll just stand down and let you make the call about what's going to happen."

Winter thought about it and nodded slowly. "That's it. That's what I think. You've done murder, but you're no murderer. You're not going to try to murder me."

Now Blake shifted, turning his body so that it was square on to Winter. "You're taking a hell of a chance, my man."

"Well," Winter said. "So are you."

There was another long, tense moment between them, gaze on gaze. Then, as if to prove his point, Winter slowly turned his back on the other. As if to give him his chance—as if to say, *Go ahead. Break my neck. You know how it's done*—he even stood still like that for a second.

Only then did he step to the cell door and call for the bailiff to release him.

18

Later, in the courtroom, Blake never looked at him. Once Blake took the witness stand, he never looked at anyone. He sat straight. Stared ahead. And again, Winter thought: Like a soldier at attention.

"I loved her." He spoke in a monotone, his pale eyes empty. "Even when I killed her, I loved her. It was because I loved her, I killed her. Because I loved her so much."

The courtroom was silent except for the quiet sound of Hester and Mrs. Atwater and some of the other women from the school weeping into their tissues.

"I was in the dark when she found me," Travis went on. "That real crazy dark you have inside yourself deep down. That little hell inside, as big as any hell there is. You don't even know it's there until you fall into it. But once you've been there, even after you come back, you always feel as if you're walking on water. Any moment, you know you can sink down into that hell again. It was Jennifer who brought me out, and I was afraid if I lost her, I would go down into the dark forever."

He paused—and though he didn't turn, didn't look at Winter or at anyone, Winter felt he saw them all, or saw him at any rate, and was gauging the reaction to what he said.

"The minute I saw that man grab hold of her in the parking lot at the beach, I knew she was his in some way. In some way, he owned her. I needed to know who he was. Why he was there. Why she let him put his hands on her like that. Because I was afraid he would take her. I was afraid he would take her away from me and I would plunge through the surface of myself and back into that dark deep down inside me. I knew if I went down this time, I would never make it back again."

It was at this point that Victoria swiveled in her seat at the defense table and looked at Winter where he was sitting in the pew just behind her. The despair in her eyes hurt him even more than her weariness. This inner darkness Travis was describing—she had seen this inner darkness in her husband's eyes when he returned from the war. She identified Travis with her husband. Robert or Richard or Roger or whatever his name was. All right, Roger. It was Roger. That's why she had wanted so much for Travis Blake to be innocent: because she identified his pain with Roger's.

"She wouldn't. Tell me. Who he was," Travis said, throwing each word down like a dagger into the dirt. "I don't know why. I only knew it was some secret. Some secret shame. Something this man had on her. Something I knew he could use to control her. Which meant he could make her go with him at any time he wanted to. I told her if she would tell me who he was, I could help. But . . ." He didn't finish the sentence. He shook his head. "It went on for months like that and then . . . Then that night, I picked up the knife, my old combat knife. I never meant to use it. Of course I didn't. I loved her, like I said. But I think in the end, it just came to me, that it would be easier that way, easier than waiting, easier than being afraid all the time. It would be easier just to have it over. The next thing I knew, the blade was buried in her chest. She was looking into my eyes and dying. Her blood was pouring, warm, onto my hand. And I loved her. Even then."

Again, the silence—silence except for the women weeping. Then the prosecutor—Jim Crawford—"Former Army Ranger Jim Crawford," as Victoria had called him—pacing under the watchful eyes of Judge Lee—"Former Army Ranger Lewis Lee"—led Travis Blake through the rest of his confession: how he cleaned the room, how he dumped her car, how he took her body rolled up in a rug down to the marina. How he sailed to the far, forested coast of the lake and sought for boulders in the woods. How he put the boulders in heavy-duty plastic bags to weigh them down. And how he then—this was the only time his voice faltered—he dismembered Jennifer's body and put the pieces in the bags with the boulders. Finally, he sailed out into the far reaches of the lake and dumped what was left of the woman he loved overboard where she would never be found. The police had looked where he told them to look but had found nothing. The truth was, he was half mad when he did it. Even he didn't really know the location.

At last, he finished his confession. He rose from the witness chair and returned to sit by Victoria at the defense table with Winter directly behind him. There followed a small procession of character witnesses, mostly the military men. They testified to Blake's patriotism, his leadership and courage. One had been among the wounded in the mountains of Nuristan when Blake had engaged in the action for which he was awarded the Silver Star. There was complete silence in the court—no crying at all—when he described how Blake, the last Ranger standing, had defended the landing field from a terrorist army until a US chopper could touch down for the extraction.

Finally, Nichola Atwater took the stand. She had stopped crying now and sat before the court composed, erect and elegant. She was the only witness to speak for Jennifer, but she said she was deputed to speak for all the people at the school who had known and loved her. They did not want vengeance on Travis Blake for what he had done, she said. They simply wanted to put on record who Jennifer had been, how remarkable she had been, how much she had changed the lives of the school's adults and children in the brief time she had been with them. She wanted the court to know how much they had lost when they lost her.

When all the witnesses were finished, Judge Lee called on Blake to stand to receive his sentence. The judge was a man of granite countenance, but he had clearly been moved by what he had heard. He spoke to the prisoner in slow, grave tones. He had been prepared, he said, to sentence Blake to life in prison without any chance of parole. But the story of Blake's heroism under fire had made him feel the prisoner had earned a chance at redemption.

"Travis Blake," he said finally. "I sentence you to prison for life, with the possibility of parole after twenty-five years."

Then he ended the hearing by smacking his gavel down upon the bench.

19

The courtroom was windowless, so when Winter stepped outside, he was startled to find that dark had fallen and it had begun to snow. The first flakes tumbled lovely out of the high shadows into the beams of the streetlights. With his hands in the pockets of his shearling coat, Winter lifted his face so he could watch the scene from under his ivy cap. After all the emotion in court, he was struck by the beauty and sadness of the world.

"It was a fair sentence," Victoria said beside him. "At least he may have some life left to live later on."

She did not sound convinced, Winter thought. It was just one of those things people say when there is nothing to say.

After another moment, he glanced at her. She was looking up at the snowfall too, as he had. He imagined she was feeling what he had: the beauty and the sadness. She had only come out of the courthouse to say goodbye to him and was wearing nothing but the dark skirt suit she had worn in court, no overcoat. She was already beginning to shiver in the cold.

"Roger will be all right," Winter told her. "Your husband. He'll be all right."

"I know who Roger is, Cameron."

Winter smiled. "He's not Blake. Each of us has a soul of his own, a life of his own, his own story. The things that happened to Blake didn't happen to Roger. He has you. You'll take care of him and he'll make it back."

She lowered her eyes to his. Shivering, she hugged herself. "Did you?" she asked. "Did you make it back?"

Winter leaned forward, put one hand on her shoulder, and went to kiss her cheek. She moved her head a little as he leaned in, and his lips touched hers at the edges. A shock of feeling went through him, a shock of physical memory. They had never been right for each other, but when it was good, it had been very good. He had a powerful sense of how wholly gone the past was, how impossible it was to recover.

He drew back, and his gaze played longingly over her face. For a second or two, she let it.

Then, tilting her head toward the courthouse door, she said: "I better get back inside. They're going to transport Travis to state prison tonight. Also, I'm freezing."

"It's been nice to see you, Vic. I'm sorry I couldn't be more help."

"We do what we can."

"Stay in touch."

He started down the steps but stopped halfway and turned back to her. She was still standing there, still hugging herself, still shivering, watching him.

"Oh," he said. "And Merry Christmas."

"You too, Cam. Do you have any place to go for the holiday?"

He shrugged. "It's never meant much to me."

He turned away before she could answer and went down the rest of the way to the sidewalk.

As he headed to his Jeep through the thickening flurry, the town's main street lay before him. In the newly gathered dark, the Christmas lights on the storefronts and the lampposts, the Santa and reindeer strung above the street, and the shoppers on their way home through the snow made for a bright and jolly scene. It could have been a small American town at the holidays of any time within the last seventy-five years. Winter admired the military discipline with which the residents had held fast to the world of tradition lest it, like the past itself, should be wholly gone, impossible to recover.

He climbed into his SUV and took one more glance out the window as he started the engine. The living Christmas panorama seemed distant from him, almost like a painted picture. His mind was still full of the things he had heard in court, the violence and the sorrow. He could not break through all that and connect with the holiday spirit.

He put the Jeep in gear and pulled away from the curb.

He headed out of town but not back to the capital, rather away, up into the hills. The snow grew steady and soon he was on small roads in the empty back country, his Jeep leaving the first tracks in the virgin white. Now and then, when he crested a hill, he could look out the window and see Sweet Haven stretched out beneath him. The Christmas lights were still visible from here. The vista seemed even more serene and timeless at a distance.

It was not hard for him to find the ruins of the old orphanage. The Sweet Haven Historical Society website had included a map of the location, and he had fed that into the GPS on his phone. He came over the last ridge and there it was. His headlights picked out the eerie silhouettes of a half-demolished mansion and a domed tower.

The building had once been a stately monument to the vigorous Christianity of its time. It was a home for abandoned children, serving all the area around. It was the project of a minister who had come over from Norway in the early nineteenth century. He supported it with ceaseless fundraising at his church and with his own businesses, a farm, a seed company, and the sale of patent medicines—all while he and his wife raised nine children.

The place had not survived the coming of modernity. The Norwegian minister died. Government welfare drained the energies of private charity. The foster system replaced the orphanage. Faith began to fail and the church grew empty. The mansion-like building had been abandoned. It fell into disrepair. It was set too far from town to be an eyesore or a danger, so no one noticed or cared when the roof caved in or even when a tornado climbed the three-thousand-foot hilltop and carried most of the main building into the surrounding nowhere. Now only the western tower with its domed roof remained intact, rising above a jagged mishmash of brick and lumber.

Winter pulled off the road onto a rocky flatland. He parked the Jeep and killed the engine. The headlights caught the falling snow, then dimmed, then died. A snow-whitened darkness shrouded everything.

Winter got out of the vehicle. His hands in his coat pockets, he walked over the freshly fallen powder to the ruin. He was not given to nerves or superstition, but even he felt the spooky weight of the black tower looming over him and the haunted silence of the empty wreckage off to his right. Beside that wreckage, the tower seemed weirdly whole and strong. Its heavy wooden door was sturdy. He rapped his knuckles sharply on the wood.

The door opened at once and there she stood before him, captured in the ghostly glow of the dim white light within. The glow made her black hair seem even blacker and her pale skin white as ivory.

Winter was not prepared for the sheer reality of her: the face he'd seen on video, the body he had fantasized about, the presence that had been described to him, the almost legendary force of her personality—all suddenly manifest in the flesh. She had not been expecting him—not him—and for a moment she stiffened in fear and surprise. But almost at once, the full truth occurred to her. She relaxed, and he saw what everyone of goodwill saw in her:

the inner stillness so complete it amounted to a kind of majesty.

"You must be Winter," she said calmly. "They told me you might come."

In an instinctive gesture, Winter removed his cap to her and felt the snow dampening his hair.

"And you," he said, "must be Jennifer Dean."

20

He found he could not take his eyes off her. When she let him in, when he followed her up the winding staircase to the little room beneath the dome, when he sat on the sofa in the small circular room, he watched her all the while, fascinated.

She moved about the makeshift kitchen filling the coffee maker with grounds and water. She was wearing jeans and a heavy dark blue sweater. Her jet-black hair had grown since the library video was filmed. It fell forward as she bent to her work, obscuring her round, sweet, feminine face. But the stillness people talked about—the inner stillness and the grace of movement—that was all there, all real, and he found it mesmerizing.

When she finally pressed the button to start the coffee maker, he forced himself to turn away before she caught him staring. He glanced around the room. The place was comfortably furnished but clumsily decorated. The blue sofa didn't go well with the green armchair, and the low table seemed a relic from a lifetime ago. But the flowery drapes around the blackout curtains were a nice touch. So was the lone decoration on the wall, a Russian icon, a Virgin with child just like the one in her apartment. It all spoke to Winter of a room set up by galumphing males with an elevated respect for women, or at least for this woman.

"Where do you get the electrics?" he asked her, gesturing at the space heater and the dim lights.

"The boys hooked me into the powerlines. They had some super military device that hides the drain from the power company."

As the coffee brewed, she faced him, leaning back against the wooden table that served as a kitchen counter.

"They warned me you were very brilliant," she said. He could hear her Russian accent, but only just. It was little more than an exotic musical undertone. "There was even a rumor you were selected from the Navy SEALs training and recruited to be a spy. Is that true?"

"I'm an English professor," Winter said.

She had a dimple on her right cheek when she smiled; very appealing. He thought perhaps she appreciated his evasion, being a master of the art herself.

"So how did you know I was here, Mr. English Professor?" she asked him. "How did you know I was just in this very place specifically?"

"We reveal ourselves in the stories we tell," Winter said—and was then annoyed to find he had quoted Margaret Whitaker without thinking. The therapist was beginning to get under his skin. "I saw the book you wrote for the children in the school library. You must have already been making your plans when you wrote it. It was a story about a dead woman who had suffered terribly and yet remained a beautiful and loving spirit, haunting a tower. Travis's sister, May, told me you and Travis used to come to this tower sometimes to be alone. I added the two facts together."

The gurgle of the coffee maker began to slow. She selected two black mugs out of a plastic container.

"I suppose I should really ask how you knew I was alive at all," she said. "It wasn't obvious, I hope."

"No, no. You did well. Travis was terrific in court today."

"Was he?"

"Even I believed him, and I knew he was lying."

She gave a deep, melodious chuckle. She poured them each a mug of coffee. "I have sugar but no milk," she told him.

"Black is fine," Winter said.

He accepted the mug from her hands, using the moment of contact to steal a direct glance at her face. The mobster Oblonsky had chosen Anya Petrovna for her beauty, and she was still beautiful, but it was more than that that held his rapt attention. How was it possible, he wondered, that she should be so still, so calm, even now—even now when he had discovered everything?

"It was when I saw Lila that I began to think about it," he told her. "You had become like a mother to her. Brought her out of her shell. Brought her father back to her. But when I saw her at May's house, she wasn't traumatized. Not at all. She was happy, laughing, not just on the surface, all the way down. She was at peace, not like a child whose mother figure had died violently at her father's hands."

Jennifer sat on the armchair. She held the coffee mug in both hands, close beneath her chin, absorbing the warmth in the chilly room. "We worried she wouldn't be able to keep the secret. Children, you know."

"No, she was very good. But it just hit me when I saw her: it was all wrong somehow. And later—I don't know. It all fell into place for me. That you were alive and she was in on the plot. That happens to me sometimes when I think about things in a certain way. They just fall into place. It's a strange habit I have."

She sipped the steam off her coffee, watching him the whole time. "And the rest?"

"Well, your friend Popov came to see me." Winter tugged his collar down so she could see the bruise on his throat.

She flinched at the sight. "Oh, I'm so sorry. Popov!"

"I gave him as good as I got," said Winter. "And at least the bullet he fired at me ended up in the wainscoting."

"Oh! Oh, Popov!" she said again.

"The feds redacted him from their reports in order to protect him," Winter said. "But I couldn't help but deduce his presence there in all those blacked-out spaces. You couldn't have drugged your guard yourself or driven yourself out of the hills after your escape. You had to have an accomplice. He's in love with you. I guess you know that."

"Poor Popov!" said Jennifer Dean. "We Russians, you see, we have believed in everything—the tsar and the church and the socialists and the capitalists—and it has all gone wrong for us, one thing after another, and now there is nothing left to believe. So we are like Oblonsky and believe in nothing except the old savageries. Or we find something true to attach our souls to . . ." She gestured toward the Madonna on the wall. "But Popov—poor Popov—he just found me."

"Yes," said Winter. "And when I realized that . . ." He paused here to drink his coffee and was startled at how good it was to feel the heat of it inside him on a cold December evening, like hot chocolate at Mia's house back in his childhood. "When I realized that, I knew it must be you he was covering for: paying Brandon Wright's rent and watching over his apartment and so forth. So then I understood: it was Brandon Wright that Travis had murdered, not you."

Still holding the coffee mug close to her, she nodded, her eyes sorrowful and far away. He could read a lot in that sorrow, a whole life of suffering and abuse.

"I begged him not to do it," Jennifer said. "I went on my knees in front of him and cried and begged him. But I loved him—I love him—and he was . . . I don't know the word. It's what you see in his eyes . . ."

"Implacable," said Winter. "He could not be moved."

"Yes, he could not be moved. And there was no other way out I could think of. I had to choose. I chose the man I love. And Lila. I chose Lila. Was that very evil of me, do you think?"

Winter only gestured vaguely.

"Yes," she said. "The Great God will have to judge me in the end."

"Wright was blackmailing you, I assume. Since he was the US Marshal who set up your new identity after you escaped Oblonsky, he was one of only three or four people who knew where you were hiding. So he blackmailed you, threatening to reveal your location to Oblonsky."

"Not just me. He blackmailed others as well. He bragged about it sometimes. He was a very bad man. He had no friends, no family. Even the Marshals Service hated him. They finally chased him out. So he was all alone. That worked to our advantage."

"Forgive me for asking, Miss Dean . . ."

"Jennifer."

"Jennifer. Forgive me for asking, but was it money he was after?"

"Oh no." She smiled sadly. "I had no money. Just enough to live on. The others he blackmailed were more successful, I think. I'm sure he wanted money from them, but not from me."

He nodded. So she had escaped from one miserable enslavement into another. She had broken out of the prison of her marriage to Oblonsky's son Grigor only to find the walls of another forced whoredom closing in—this one run by the US Marshal who was supposed to protect her. Winter had to shake off the image of Brandon Wright's mutilated face hovering over her.

"I bore it, at first," she said, gazing off into the room's shadows. "You can, you know, if you have to. Bear things, I mean. Especially knowing what Oblonsky would do to me if he ever found me. He had described it all in such detail. So I bore it. But somehow, it wasn't enough for Brandon. After a time, he grew angry with me. He became abusive, violent."

"Of course he did," said Winter. "Because he couldn't have you. Not really. Not completely, the way he wanted."

"Yes, I suppose it was something like that. I was afraid eventually he would kill me. Because I would never let him have me. Not really. Yes."

"So you escaped again. I'm guessing it was your old friend Popov who helped you build a new identity. Jennifer Dean."

"We are very good at identities, we Russians. Very thorough. Almost as good as the US government."

"Then you came here. And tried to keep to yourself. But you fell in love, first with Lila, then with Travis."

The coffee mug was at her lips again so that when she sighed, the steam blew away to nothing. Winter had a clear view of her eyes and how calm they were, even now.

"And then Brandon Wright found you again," he said. "He must have been obsessed."

"Yes," she said. "I think he was. Obsessed—yes. And he was very good at what he did. Tracking people—that was his whole job. That's what he was trained for and he was excellent at it. He told me: there was nowhere I could ever go that he would not find me. And I believed him."

"And he wanted you back," said Winter.

"And now, you see, I couldn't bear it. Not anymore. Now there was Travis. Now there was Lila. I just couldn't go back to him."

"Of course you couldn't," said Winter. There was sympathy in his voice, and it was real sympathy. Which was the best he could offer her. He wasn't going to tell her what he thought of Brandon Wright or make a display of his righteous anger to her. The anger boiled inside him, but this was no time for sentimentality. They were still talking about murder, after all.

"I tried not to tell Travis. I knew what he would do. But when I told Brandon I would not return to our old arrangement . . ." She shook her head. "I don't want to make any excuses for myself."

"I won't take it that way."

"Well, soon after, soon after I refused, Popov contacted me. He'd never done that before. But he was in a panic. He was calling to tell me that Brandon had carried out his threat. He had sold my information to Oblonsky. Oblonsky knew where I was now. And he was sending a gunman to find me. He was planning a terrible revenge."

Winter put his coffee mug down on the low table. He leaned forward, elbows on his knees, looking at her openly now, openly entranced. She was like her own Russian icon, he thought, a lady of majesty and sorrow, ill-used but unbeaten, wonderfully herself.

"Let me see if I've worked it out," he said. "After Popov warned you that Oblonsky was sending a gunman to get you, you confessed the whole thing to Travis."

"I had to. I was so afraid. Not just for me. For Lila too. And even for Travis. I'd sent Oblonsky's son to prison for life. There was no end to what he'd do to hurt me." She shook her head. Her eyes filled, but the tears did not fall over. "I wanted to run. I begged Travis to run away with me but . . ."

"Where could you have gone? Like you said, Wright was a professional tracker and he'd never stop looking. You'd never have felt safe. And it wasn't just your life at risk now. There was Travis and Lila too."

"Yes," said Jennifer. "That's what Travis said. They would have made me watch as they killed them."

"But why couldn't you leave Brandon Wright alive?" said Winter. "Why not just fake your death and leave town?"

She nearly cried out her answer: "Because the whole thing was his idea!" Winter recoiled a little, surprised. She went on: "That was what he said to me at the beach that day. 'Wherever you go, I'll find you. Whatever I hear, I'll keep looking. Fake your death, I won't believe it. Even if you kill yourself, I'll follow you to hell.' "

Winter sat back in the sofa, covered his face with his hands, and laughed. It was an inappropriate sound, he knew, mirthless as it was, quick as it was. But he couldn't help it. Wright had condemned himself by the power of his own corrupt obsession. *Fake your death, I won't believe it.* Of course Blake would have to kill him if he wanted his Jennifer to be free at last.

He dropped his hands into his lap. "So Travis—what? I'm guessing he contacted Wright and told him he would pay him a lot of money if Wright would just leave you alone."

Jennifer nodded. "Brandon was greedy. He saw a chance to make even more money off me, to get paid double, once by Oblonsky and once by Travis."

"He knew he would have to act quickly, though," Winter said. "He had to get his hands on Travis's money before Oblonsky's gunman reached you and revealed there was no reason to pay him off anymore. Haste made him sloppy and careless, right? That's why he agreed to meet Travis—where? Somewhere by the lake."

"Yes. There's a forest by the shore about a hundred miles from here," said Jennifer. "Brandon was a fool to go, but he wanted that money."

"So Wright met Travis in the forest by the lake to get his big payoff, and Travis killed him. And the rest . . ."

"The rest was just like acting out a play," Jennifer said.

"Acting out a play," Winter echoed. "Inventing a motive. Designing a scenario. Your blood on Travis's knife. Your car in the river. Your body in the rug caught on camera. Then he took you out on his boat and sailed across the water to the forest. Dropped you off and picked up Wright's body and dumped Wright in the lake, not you."

"He worked all night. He even took Brandon's car apart and sank the pieces. But no one was looking for Brandon's car. No one was looking for Brandon. He was a solitary man."

"So now all you had to do was get Popov to help out with the apartment, keep anyone from realizing Wright was missing."

"When the lease runs out, Popov will simply move the furniture and pretend his so-called father has gone to Florida. No one on earth will ever miss him. They may never even find out he's dead."

"I guess Popov panicked when I came by."

"We had warned him how smart you were," Jennifer said. "He's a fool when it comes to me."

"Other than that, it was pretty much flawless. Brandon Wright was no longer a threat. And with your murder publicized and proved at trial, Oblonsky's man would stand down. They would never suspect it was a fake. How could it be a fake when Blake was sentenced to life in prison? It was perfect. For the first time—the first time since you'd been kidnapped as a girl—you were completely free."

"Completely free," she murmured.

After that, for a moment, there was silence between them—silence except for the whir of the space heater. And maybe something else as well—something outside. Maybe it was just Winter's imagination, but he could have sworn he heard a car engine in the distance, a car straining up the hill in the snow.

"The life sentence—that was the genius of it," he told her. "That was the one part I couldn't figure out for the longest time. How could you—a woman like you—let Travis go to prison for you—how could you let him go to prison for life to buy your freedom? And how could he let himself go and leave his daughter behind? It didn't fit. It was totally out of character for both of you."

She smiled slightly but said nothing. She wasn't drinking her coffee anymore. It was probably cold by now, Winter thought. But she went on holding the mug in her two hands as if there was still some warmth in it. She continued gazing at nothing, and Winter couldn't help but spend the next few seconds in a long study of her, her hands, her hair, her face. It was not that he was in love with her, he told himself. This was, he told himself again, no time for sentimentality. It was just: he could have loved her. He was sure of that. He knew there weren't that many women that a man like him could love, and she was one of them.

"Finally, I got it," he went on. "Your supposed murder—like you said, it was a kind of play, a kind of story you were telling. We reveal ourselves in our stories. And finally, it occurred to me: this whole town is a kind of story. Sweet Haven is a story the soldiers tell when they retire. About the country they left, the country they fought for, the country they want this to be again. And I suddenly asked myself: What if you were all telling the same story? You and Travis and all the old soldiers—or whichever soldiers Travis decided he could trust. The judge certainly. The prosecutor. All the jailers and the bailiffs. Just about everyone in the legal system here except for poor Victoria. She was left out of it because you couldn't be sure she'd play along. She sensed something was wrong but she couldn't put it together. That's why she came to me."

Jennifer shifted her gaze now and looked at him directly—looked at him with all that grace and sorrow and stillness until he thought his feelings for her would break his heart.

"And so you played out the play," he said hoarsely. "Everyone played out the play. Blake was arrested. He confessed. He was sentenced to life. And off they took him to the state prison. Except then—what? An accident? A daring break? Some sort of escape scenario, right? Maybe they'll even fake his death, too, eventually. Maybe they'll find his body in a couple of days. Why not? It's a military operation. They can pretty much do anything they want. Travis Blake will escape on his way to prison—he's probably already escaped even now. And one of his Ranger buddies—maybe the friend who was going to pick up Lila at May's—was waiting to pick him up too, somewhere nearby."

She didn't have to tell him he was right. He was certain now. And no, he hadn't imagined it: there was a car approaching. He got a faint glimpse of the headlights in a small gap between the blackout curtains and the wall. From the tone of the engine, it sounded as if it was almost at the top of the hill.

"Well . . ." said Winter. She barely looked at him as he stood up. He paused over her and fetched his ivy cap from his coat pocket. He put it on, pulling the brim low. "Thank you for the coffee, Jennifer."

She said nothing. He walked to the top of the winding staircase.

Then she couldn't help herself. She blurted out: "Mr. Winter—please . . . !" But when he turned to face her, she went silent again. She shook her head. "No. No, I won't beg you to let us get away."

Again, he marveled at the stillness in her, the peace in her eyes, even now.

"In heaven, the Great God will judge me," she said. "But here on earth, I must leave it to you."

21

Winter stepped out of the tower just as the big black SUV—a Ford Explorer—rumbled over the top of the hill, its headlights brightening the falling snow. The Ford pulled up beside Winter's Jeep. And even before the vehicle came to a full stop, Travis Blake was stepping out through the rear door. Winter caught a glimpse of the little girl still sitting inside. He saw the shadows of the two large men up in front.

Blake confronted him, his body rigid, his face alight with fear and anger. He had not thought he would find him here. He had not thought he would guess this, the location.

Before the two men could exchange a word, Blake's glance shifted to look over Winter's shoulder.

Winter knew Jennifer had come into the doorway behind him.

A second later, the little girl burst out of the SUV. "Jennifer!"

Winter turned and saw the woman and the child rush together. Jennifer knelt in the snow to wrap her arms around the girl. The snow came down on both of them, lit by the outglow from the Ford's headlights. Travis Blake moved to join them, and the three clung together for a long moment.

Winter watched them. More than that, he was lost in the sight of them. He was surprised by how much the reunion affected him. It touched him. It made him feel heartsore and terribly lonely. He could almost feel the woman and the girl in his arms—his arms instead of Blake's—as if it were he they loved. A man, a woman, and a child, he thought. What an elemental thing it was, when you came down to it. Everything else was just passing through. Like Winter: just passing through.

It was in that state of mind—that state of emotional solitude, of alienation, of estrangement from the elemental things—that he came to his decision. In that moment, he felt no loyalty to anything but the truth of what had happened here. He had no outlook, no philosophy, no interest, no tradition. He had only what was in front of him: a man, a woman, and a child, and the truth. Everything seemed very clear finally. He knew now what he was going to do.

The sound of car doors opening drew him from his thoughts. When he turned back to the SUV, he saw the two other men rising out of the front seats. They came around the vehicle and moved to stand together, about a foot apart, both hatless, oblivious to the snowfall. One was a tall, thick, powerful white man with a shaggy red beard. The other was a tall, thick, powerful black man with a shaggy black beard. Tier One military killing machines, Winter had no doubt. And they were looking at him—*balefully,* he thought, would be the right word.

Travis Blake now stepped away from his little group and moved back toward Winter. Jennifer went on holding Lila, stroking her hair, murmuring comfort to her.

Blake came close. Winter met his gaze. One corner of his mouth lifted. He tilted his head at the two other men.

"They could do the job for you, no question," he said.

"They could," said Blake. He let the words hang there for a long second. Then he added: "But you're right, Winter. I'm not a murderer."

"Yes. I know."

Blake hesitated then. Winter watched him as an inner struggle played itself out on his features. Then Blake said: "Give us an hour head start, Winter. That's all I need." Winter could see it hurt his pride to ask even for this. But for the sake of the woman and the child, he did ask for it, and he said, "I did what I had to do. I know it was murder under the law but—"

"I'm not the law, Travis," Winter broke in. "The law would have to condemn you. I don't. You snuffed out a blackmailer who raped your girl. I'd've done the same. I'd've killed him and then brought him back to life so I could kill him again. I'm not turning you in. Not now. Not ever. I'll never even tell this story. It ends with me." He lifted his face to the snowfall. "Anyway," he said. "It's Christmas. Get the hell out of here. I won't stop you. Travel safe."

He heard Jennifer Dean cry out. She ran across the snow to Winter. She threw her arms around him. She pressed her face against his face. He felt her tears dampening his cheek. He would have liked her to stay like that for a long time, maybe forever.

"The Great God will bless you for this!" she whispered to him.

Winter smiled. He was not entirely convinced of the Great God's benevolent feelings toward him, but he figured if the Great God was there at all, he was likely to give special consideration to the prayers of Jennifer Dean.

When she released him, Blake offered him his hand. Winter shook it.

"Take care of them, Blake," he said.

"Count on it," said Travis Blake.

They broke off the handshake, but Winter lingered. He didn't know why. In his imagination, he could still feel Jennifer's face pressed against his. Maybe it was that. Maybe he didn't want to walk away from that feeling. He smiled down at Lila, who now looked up at him wide-eyed, clinging to Jennifer's leg.

Then he said to Blake, "Do you know where you'll go?"

Blake nodded slowly. "Another country," he said. "A foreign country."

Winter, the literary man, gave a soft puff of air. It turned to steam in the cold weather. "Well," he said. "I hope you find what you're looking for."

With that, he put one finger to his cap in a brief salute to the two giants who had been waiting for the opportunity to pound him to atoms. He gave them a wide berth as he walked around the Ford to his Jeep. He was glad to slide behind the wheel, to get out of the cold.

He had one more glimpse of them as he pulled the Jeep out: three figures captured in the headlights, a child clinging to a woman, a man with his arm around the woman's shoulders, the snow coming down on them, man, woman, and child, like figures in a Christmas globe. For the last time, he let himself imagine the pressure of her cheek against his cheek, and he felt that rush of loneliness again, not for the last time.

Then he turned the Jeep around and headed down the mountain.

EPILOGUE

I went to see Charlotte on Christmas Eve. I went to the house where she'd been living. I had to call Mia to find out her last address. It was a very sad phone call. She's old now—Mia. She sort of rambles and reminisces. Her sister is bedridden. Albert is gone. It sounded to me like he drank himself to death.

And Charlotte—she says Charlotte never calls her anymore. The last address she had for her was six years old. Still in Indiana. Still in the same town, in fact, the college town. She said she thought Eddie the evil troll was out of the picture now, but she wasn't sure.

So I drove out there. Like I said, it was Christmas Eve. There was no one in the city anyway. I had nowhere else to go.

I arrived at about five in the evening. It was a dark day, and dusk was already far advanced. The streets were covered with snow, and there was a light snow falling. I went to the address. It was a nice neighborhood. A nice house, a neat little traditional brick house with a good-size lawn in front and lots of trees around. There were kids making a snowman a few houses over. It seemed a tranquil family neighborhood.

I parked on the street outside and just watched the house for a while. With the dark gathering, with the lights on inside and the curtains open, I could see right in. I could see the Christmas tree through the picture window, a five-foot fir in the living room lovingly trimmed with lights and ornaments. There was a fire in the fireplace. Greenery strung along the mantelpiece. Christmas stockings hung there. Candles lit and glowing. Off to the right, through a side window, I could see a long table all prepared in the dining room. Eight places set. Ready for a family gathering.

After a while, I saw a woman come in. I guess she came out of the kitchen. She was wearing a frilly white blouse and a green skirt and a Christmas apron, red and white. She was carrying a tray. She was clearly the mistress of the house. Pretty, like a picture in an advertisement, like a wife on an old TV show. She brought the tray into the living room and set it down. I could see she was not Charlotte.

A man came into the room and joined her, a young man about her own age, her husband, I guess. He was wearing a Christmas sweater. He had a big black beard. He said something to her and she laughed and he kissed her. They seemed a happy couple. A happy couple waiting for family to come for dinner on Christmas Eve. Like a picture in an advertisement.

But Charlotte was gone. Assuming she had ever been there, assuming this was the right address in the first place. I thought of knocking on the door and asking if they knew where she had moved to, but it seemed an intrusion. Christmas Eve with family coming and all.

I don't know what it is about houses at night—houses with lighted windows in the dark of night—they always make me feel sad somehow, as if I'm lost out in the world alone and everyone else is safe and warm and together inside. I sat there and watched for a few minutes more, then I left.

I made the drive back, a long drive back, listening to Christmas music all the way, the old songs like we used to play at Mia's house when I was a child. It was only nine o'clock or so when I got home. When I pulled up at the garage to my building, as I was waiting for the gate to open, I saw a man coming out the front door, a man I recognized. He was a big man, tall, thick, and powerful, with a shaggy red beard. A top-tier soldier. I could tell that just by looking at him. And, as I say, I'd seen him before.

I wondered what he was doing there. I watched as he crossed the street to his Ford Explorer—as he got in and drove away. Then the gate to the garage rattled open and I went in.

I took the elevator up to my floor. The moment I entered my apartment, I saw why the man had come. I saw what he had left me. There was an envelope lying just inside the threshold, one of those greeting card envelopes, bright red. The man had obviously slid it under the door. I opened it up and there was a Christmas card inside. Nothing fancy. Just a standard card with a manger scene. Three kings, the shepherds, the barn animals—all of them gathered around the family at the center: the man, the woman, and the child. There was a printed message: "Rejoice evermore!"

That was all. There was no signature, but I knew who it was from. It was from another man, woman, and child—another family in another country. A foreign country. I had done them a favor once, and I guess they wanted to thank me. To thank me and to let me know they were all right now.

So that was how I spent my Christmas Eve. Holding that card—that card and a stiff whiskey. Sitting in my armchair by the window to my terrace, looking out at the snow falling over the city.

It was lonely, but it was pleasant to think about them. My friends, I mean, the ones who sent me the card. It was pleasant to think that they were all right, that they were going about their business, making a new family in a new place. A man, a woman, and a child. It's such an elemental thing.

And it was, it really was nice to imagine them, wherever they were. It made me feel that somewhere out there, the world was beginning again.

ACKNOWLEDGMENTS

My deep thanks to the great Otto Penzler for suggesting I write a Christmas novella, thereby giving me a chance to tell a story that had been in my mind for decades. My thanks to Charles Perry and the team at Mysterious Press, who saw the book into print with remarkable skill and efficiency. Thank you too to Mark Gottlieb and everyone at Trident Media Group for seeing the deal through. Thanks as well to Jenna Ellis, who graciously answered my persistent questions about legal procedures—which allowed me to then bend the procedures out of shape for storytelling purposes. Thank you to my daughter Faith Moore and my son Spencer Klavan for reading a draft. And as always—and always as deeply—my thanks to my wife Ellen Treacy, for everything, and for all the Christmases.